Sam took a deep breath and stood up extra straight,

grinning out at the crowd for all she was worth.

"Sam Bridges is five-feet, ten-inches," Mrs. Spangler said. "She has red hair and blue eyes. She stays fit by dancing—with her friends, with her boyfriend, even alone. Sam just loves to dance!"

She turned slowly so the judges could look at her from behind, then she looked over her shoulder and pivoted, just as Lord Owen had taught in his seminar.

Just at that moment she felt something snap at her hip. Without stopping to think, she reached down and felt the fabric, which was just about to rip. She held the fabric in place and continued to smile. Then she felt the same snap on the other side, and she grabbed that material, too.

I can't believe this is happening to me, Sam thought in a panic, though she kept the same huge smile on her face. If I drop my hands, my bathing suit is going to fall off. I've got to do something!

Sunset Passion

CHERIE BENNETT

Sunset™ Island

SPLASH™

A BERKLEY / SPLASH BOOK

SUNSET PASSION is an original publication of The Berkley Publishing Group. This work has never appeared before in book form.

SUNSET PASSION

A Berkley Book / published by arrangement with General Licensing Company, Inc.

PRINTING HISTORY
Berkley edition / November 1994

A GLC BOOK

Splash and *Sunset Island* are trademarks belonging to General Licensing Company, Inc.

ISBN: 0-425-14397-X

BERKLEY®
Berkley Books are published by
The Berkley Publishing Group,
200 Madison Avenue, New York, New York 10016.
BERKLEY and the "B" design
are trademarks belonging to Berkley Publishing Corporation.

PRINTED IN THE UNITED STATES OF AMERICA

10 9 8 7 6 5 4 3 2 1

For Jeff,
a Steven Seagal lookalike,
only cuter

Sunset Passion

ONE

"That girl is beautiful!" four-year-old Katie Hewitt breathed, her eyes glued to the TV set in Graham Perry Templeton's massive family room.

"No, she isn't," five-year-old Chloe Templeton insisted. "She's got fat legs."

"Oh, yeah, you're right," Katie said, scrutinizing the TV more closely. "And her nose looks like Miss Piggy's, if you ask me."

"Maybe we shouldn't be judging these girls solely on the basis of their looks," Carrie Alden said gently to the two little girls.

"Right," her best friend, Emma Cresswell, agreed. "Maybe that girl is a really nice person."

1

The children stared at their au pairs as if they were both crazy.

"But, Carrie," Chloe said slowly, as if she were talking to a particularly slow adult, "this is a beauty pageant. That's what you're supposed to do!"

Samantha Bridges, the third member of the trio of best friends, threw herself back on the couch and laughed. "I guess she told you, Carrie!" Sam hooted. She reached for another handful of Doritos. "I've discovered the secret to babysitting heaven. Put a beauty pageant on television. It stops any girl under the age of eight in her tracks."

The annual Miss Galaxy beauty pageant was on television, and Sam, Emma, and Carrie were hanging out in the Templetons' enormous family room watching it with Chloe and Katie.

Carrie and Emma had arranged a sleepover for the two little girls, who had become good friends that summer, and Sam had joined them, since her boss, Dan Jacobs, had given her the night off. When the

2

pageant had come on, Katie and Chloe had begged to watch.

"Eww, that one is a dog!" Chloe cried, pointing to the screen.

"Ruff, ruff!" Katie agreed, making barking noises.

Carrie sighed. "This is not exactly the healthiest way for these two kids to look at women," she said.

"Oh, lighten up," Sam said, picking up her Coke. "Whoa, check out the hooters on Miss India!"

"Sam!" Emma chided, nudging her friend in the ribs.

Chloe turned around and looked at Sam. "I want to have big ones when I grow up," she said seriously.

Sam cracked up and pushed some of her wild red curls behind her ears. "Unfortunately, you don't get to put in a special order, or I would be the first one in line!"

"You're a total fox and you know it," Carrie said.

"Yes," Sam agreed, "but I'm a flat-chested fox."

"Ssssh!" Katie hissed, without taking her eyes off the television. "We're watching!"

"Anything to keep them quiet," Sam joked. "I'll shut up."

She leaned back on the couch and closed her eyes for a moment, content just to be doing nothing and having fun with her two best friends.

We've been fighting so much lately, Sam thought, *that it's just so great we can be hanging out and goofing around. And what we were fighting about was so dumb!*

For about the millionth time, Sam considered with happy surprise the amazing circumstances that had brought her, Emma, and Carrie together on Sunset Island, and then turned them into best friends.

Not only were the three of them spending their second straight summer on fabulous Sunset Island, the world-famous resort island at the far reaches of Casco Bay off the coast of Portland, Maine, but they were still best friends.

And they were all so different from one another. Sam thought this was the most amazing thing of all. Sam had been born and raised in Junction, Kansas, and was a tall, thin redhead with lots of style and an outrageous sense of humor. Carrie, the daughter of two doctors, was going into her sophomore year at Yale, and was dark-haired, dark-eyed, and very curvaceous—Carrie thought *too* curvaceous.

And Emma, Sam thought, *Emma's the most unlikely one of us all to be working as an au pair, taking care of kids for a family.* Emma was a Boston heiress with perfect, patrician blond hair and features—actually, perfect everything. And while every female member of the Cresswell family had been a French major at Goucher College in Maryland, it was Emma's dream to join the Peace Corps someday and study primates in Africa.

How the three of us met at the International Au Pair Convention in New York and got to be best friends should be a movie, Sam thought. *And I should play myself in it!*

"You guys want anything to eat?" Carrie asked the kids.

5

"Ssssh!" Both little girls shushed Carrie at once.

"We're watching," Katie said.

"Yeah," Chloe seconded.

"She's pretty," Katie commented as Miss Zambia paraded across the television screen.

"She's prettier," Chloe said, watching Miss Zimbabwe do her introductory walk and then stop to deliver a few words directly into the camera.

"I'm Lindsay Chumunga, and I'm proud to be here in Manila tonight, representing my country, Zimbabwe!" She then flashed a two-thousand-watt smile at the camera.

"Get me my sunglasses," Sam joked. "Where is Zimbabwe, anyway?" she asked. "South America somewhere?"

"Southern Africa," Carrie said, reaching for her Diet Coke.

"That was my next guess," Sam said huffily, but then she grinned widely. "Anyway, Emma will soon be sending us postcards from somewhere around there."

"I have to do another year of college before the Peace Corps will even consider me," Emma sighed.

"Maybe you'll be married to Kurt by then," Sam said slyly.

"I just hope we're together," Emma said. "It hasn't been easy, you know, trying to patch things up after everything that's happened—"

"Emma, be quiet!" Katie commanded her au pair. "I missed what the announcer said!"

"It's a commercial, Katie," Carrie pointed out.

"So?" Katie said. "It's about stuff that makes your hair shiny. I wanted to hear it."

Carrie shook her head. "This is creepy. Were we like that when we were kids?"

"I was worse," Sam admitted. "I wanted to wear makeup when I was five."

"Does your deodorant hold up on the job?" a middle-aged woman was asking her officemate on the TV.

"*Mute!*" Chloe screamed.

Automatically, Sam found the remote control and cut off the sound.

Amazing, Sam chuckled to herself. *The*

7

kid was probably born knowing about the mute button and when to use it.

"You're bumming out advertisers all over the world, Sam," Carrie said, helping herself to a handful of Doritos.

"Hey!" Chloe Templeton said. "Watch me!"

Chloe rushed into the hallway, then came sashaying back into the family room swaying her hips, perfectly imitating the walk of one of the Miss Galaxy contestants.

"Bravo!" Emma cried.

"Three-hundred points!" Carrie chimed in.

"Hey, is this beauty pageant fixed? Did you kiss one of the judges?" Sam teased the little girl.

"I didn't!" Chloe shrieked. "I'm Miss Galaxy because I'm the prettiest!"

"No way!" Katie said, jumping to her feet and prancing around the room in perfect imitation of Chloe's perfect imitation. "*I* am!"

"No! *Me!*" Chloe yelled.

"Uh-uh!" Katie retorted.

Uh-oh, junior crisis erupting here, Sam

thought as the two girls' voices escalated. *Time to save the day and prevent further bloodshed.*

"We'll be holding the finals later!" Sam announced. "Now look! It's back on!" She pointed to the television, where the contest had resumed. "You guys gotta watch the whole thing, right?"

Instantly, both little girls resumed their positions in front of the big-screen TV and quieted right down.

"Nice work," Emma complimented Sam. "They did exactly what you told them to do."

"Yeah," Sam agreed. "Now, if only I had that kind of power over guys!"

For the next hour the older girls laughed and joked, and the little girls kept shushing them.

"Ladies and gentlemen," the emcee finally said, "it's time to announce our four Miss Galaxy finalists. In no particular order, they are . . . Miss United States! Miss Costa Rica! Miss Indonesia! Miss India!"

"You mean I have to keep watching the one with the hooters?" Sam asked.

"Apparently," Carrie noted.

The four finalists, clad in their evening gowns, took one last parade walk down the runway to thunderous applause from the crowd.

"Get a load of the gown on Miss United States!" Sam said loudly. "Who designed that monstrosity?" Miss United States was wearing a red, white, and blue sequined gown with ruffles of red over her bosom and up the side slit that ran nearly to her waist. "Tacky to the max! She's committing a fashion crime in our national colors!"

Sam picked up a rubber band that happened to be lying on the coffee table and fired it at the TV.

"Two points!" Sam crowed. "Direct hit!"

"Ssssh!" Chloe Templeton cried. "You're being so immature!"

Carrie and Emma couldn't stop themselves from laughing at that. Sam threw a pillow at them before turning her attention back to the TV, where the emcee was explaining how the finals would work. The finalists would be taken offstage to a special soundproof booth. Then, one at a time, each finalist would be escorted to center stage, where she would be asked a single question selected by the panel of judges.

"Their answers to this question," the emcee said, "will determine who wins this year's Miss Galaxy crown!"

"Ask 'em who they like better, Pearl Jam or Alice in Chains, and why," Sam quipped.

"I don't think so," Carrie laughed.

"Sssssh!" Katie and Chloe said at the same time.

The first contestant out was Miss Indonesia. She walked confidently across the stage.

"Miss Indonesia," the emcee asked, "what is the essence of womanhood?"

"To be in Presley Travis's arms on a hot summer night," Sam stated.

"In my opinion," Miss Indonesia answered, as if she'd been totally prepared for this question, "the essence of womanhood is

11

motherhood. To be a mother, to bring children into this world, to be a good wife—this is the essence of womanhood."

"Gag me," Sam commented.

"Well, she has a point," Emma replied. "In some ways, anyway."

"Please," Sam groaned. "She said that only because the judges eat that junk up."

The next contestant out was Miss United States. The emcee asked her the same question, and Miss United States gave just about the same answer as had Miss Indonesia.

"What is this?" Sam asked. "A conspiracy? Did they give them their lines backstage?"

"Ssssh!" Chloe hissed.

"The essence of womanhood is to follow your dreams, to be a good person, to learn and grow," Carrie stated simply. "Just like the essence of manhood. What a stupid, sexist question."

"The essence of manhood for you, Carrie," Sam joked, "is Billy Sampson!"

"Billy," Carrie sighed. Her boyfriend had returned home to Seattle recently after his father had been in a major accident. "He called me last night, and—"

"Be quiet!" Katie yelled. "This is the good part!"

Miss India had just finished—giving a variation on the same answer—and Miss Costa Rica walked to center stage.

"Miss Costa Rica has asked that she be permitted to answer the question in her native language, which is Spanish."

An offscreen voice then asked the question in rapid-fire Spanish. Miss Costa Rica considered for a moment, and gave her reply.

Emma made a face.

"What'd she say?" Sam demanded.

"What do you think?" Emma asked.

"Ladies and gentlemen," the emcee announced, "the judges have totaled their scores and we have our Miss Galaxy."

"This is so beat!" Sam exclaimed. "They're like clones! They all answered the question exactly the same way!"

"Ssssh!" everyone in the room hissed at Sam.

13

"The third runner-up," the announcer said portentously, "is . . . Miss United States. The second runner-up . . . Miss Costa Rica! And the new Miss Galaxy is . . . Miss India!"

"Hurrah!" Chloe and Katie cheered, and got up to sashay around the room doing their beauty pageant walk again.

"Figures," Sam said glumly.

"What do you mean?" Carrie asked.

"The judges are mostly men, right?" Sam asked.

"I think so," Emma said.

"So it figures," Sam declared. "When all else is equal, they pick the one with the major hooters!"

"You're a cynic," Emma told her, getting up from the couch to stretch. "Hey, kids, how about if we all help clean up in here, okay?"

"Okay," Chloe said. "What should we do?"

"Why don't you girls carry the empty glasses into the kitchen and put them in the dishwasher?" Carrie suggested.

The little girls dutifully took the glasses

and padded into the kitchen. Carrie gathered up the pages of the *Breakers,* the Sunset Island newspaper, that had gotten strewn around the room. When she picked up the front page something caught her eye. "Hey, look at this," she told her friends.

"What?" Emma asked as she and Sam peered over Carrie's shoulder.

MISS SUNSET ISLAND PAGEANT
TO BE HELD ON ISLAND

All girls between the ages of eighteen and twenty-four are invited to enter the first Miss Sunset Island beauty pageant. Nationally known celebrities will be judging this event. Contestants will be judged on beauty, fitness, talent, poise, and self-expression. The winner will receive a two-thousand-dollar savings bond, a scholarship worth three thousand dollars, and other prizes and services. Interested girls can call Mrs. Spangler at 555-7789 for registration information. Sponsored by Pageants International and the Sunset Island Chamber of Commerce.

"Whoa, baby!" Sam yelped. "This must be our lucky day!"

Carrie gave her a look. "You mean you'd actually enter this thing?"

"No, I mean I'd actually *win* this thing! Major bucks, lots of other stuff, I'm there!" Sam cried.

"But it's so . . . so . . ." Emma couldn't seem to find the word she wanted to say.

"Beneath you, O Ice Princess of the North?" Sam teased.

"No, not that," Emma said. "Embarrassing. That's it. I'd feel embarrassed and ridiculous. I don't even *like* beauty pageants."

"You don't see guys parading around in teeny bathing suits while we judge them," Carrie pointed out.

"No," Sam agreed, "but I'd really like to. Listen, you guys, I'm tall, I'm cute, I'm talented, and I'm gonna go for it! What have I got to lose?"

"Sorry, Sam," Katie piped up from the doorway. "But I don't think you'll win."

"Me, neither," Chloe agreed.

Sam felt a sting of hurt, even though she

knew it was ridiculous. "Why not?" she asked the little girls.

Katie and Chloe looked at each other, then looked back at Sam. "No major hooters!" they both declared.

Then they ran out of the room, shrieking and laughing at the top of their lungs.

TWO

"You're fabulous, you're a fox, you're everything," Sam told her reflection as she fluffed up her hair in the mirror one last time.

It was the next afternoon, and she was on her way to meet Mrs. Spangler to sign up for the Miss Sunset Island beauty pageant. She had called that morning, and had been told where and when to register.

Sam had dressed carefully, and had applied her makeup as if every swipe of the mascara wand counted. *It's never too early to make a great impression,* she thought as she applied some matte red lipstick.

She turned her back to the mirror and looked at her reflection over her shoulder, then turned around again. She'd chosen a short, pleated black-and-white checked skirt with a white tank top and a black-on-black embroidered vest, and of course her trademark red cowboy boots. For Sam this outfit was ordinary, even conservative. But then, Sam often created her own clothes from fabric remnants and old rhinestone pins.

"Lookin' good, sweet thang," she told herself, imitating the Tennessee drawl of her boyfriend, Pres.

"It's a sign of early senility when you talk to yourself, you know," fourteen-year-old Becky Jacobs said from the doorway to Sam's room. Allie stood next to her twin, leaning against the doorframe.

"I'm getting myself psyched, that's all," Sam told her.

"Well, this is totally unfair, if you ask me," Allie groused. "I mean, why should you have to be eighteen to enter this thing? Answer me that!"

"I don't make the rules," Sam said, spraying some Sunset Magic perfume through her hair. She smiled at her reflection, testing out her cuteness factor.

"You've got lipstick on your teeth and it's gross," Becky told her.

"You're so helpful," Sam said sarcastically, wiping at her front teeth with her finger. "How's that?"

"Better," Becky allowed. "Listen, will you ask the beauty pageant lady if she'll lower the age on this thing? I mean, why start at eighteen? Eighteen is like, past prime time, you know?"

"Gee, I don't exactly think of myself as over the hill," Sam replied, looking around for her purse.

"It's on the door handle," Allie said, passing it over to Sam. "So, how late will you have to stay at this meeting?"

"It's not a meeting," Sam replied. "It's just registration. Maybe they need to see us so they can weed out girls who are hopeless, I don't know." She hoisted the strap of her purse over her shoulder.

"Don't forget to bring home a pizza for dinner," Allie said. "No pepperoni."

"And some chocolate ice cream," Becky added.

"I'm glad to hear you're done with that stupid diet," Sam said as she brushed by them and headed for the stairs.

"I've got my period. I need junk food," Allie explained.

"Me, too," Becky echoed.

"Hey, I can relate," Sam agreed. "Except I need junk food all the time. So, wish me luck."

"Yeah, whatever," Becky said, her arms folded petulantly. "I still think we ought to be able to enter."

Give it a rest, Sam sighed to herself as she went downstairs. Then she looked back up at the twins. "By the way, are you guys going out tonight?"

"Dad is making us go to the movies with him and Kiki," Becky said, sticking her finger down her throat to illustrate what she thought of that prospect.

"Sorry," Sam sang out, but inside she was exultant. *Too cool! That means I'm free to go out with Pres and Emma and Kurt! Which beats an evening with the monsters anytime!*

The first people Sam saw when she walked into the large conference room at the Sunset Inn were Lorell Courtland and Diana De Witt, her archenemies.

Ah, the two girls who live to make my life a thing of misery, Sam thought as she eyed the two of them standing together a few feet away.

Lorell had been off the island for a couple of weeks. As for Diana, the last time Sam had seen her she'd been a total wreck because she thought she was pregnant. It had been too early for her to take a home pregnancy test, but she had all the symptoms.

"Why, Sammi!" Lorell cried in her sickeningly sweet Southern drawl when she caught sight of Sam. "You can't possibly be here for the beauty pageant, can you?"

"No, Lorell, I came to welcome you back to the island," Sam deadpanned. "All the joy in my life disappeared when you left."

Lorell trilled a high, tinkly laugh. "Well, I missed you, too, Sammi. After all, just seeing you is good for a laugh a day!"

Sam looked over at Diana, and noted that Diana looked much better than she had the last time she'd seen her.

But she's got that same old bitchy look on her face, Sam thought. When Diana had confided in her about her recent pregnancy scare, Sam had thought she and Diana might be beginning to get along. *She's still acting like she's so much better than me. Why did I ever think she had changed?*

"How are you?" Sam asked Diana.

"Fine, of course," Diana said sharply. "I'm always fine."

"Not recently," Sam said pointedly.

"Oh, that," Diana said, shaking her chestnut curls. "False alarm."

"But you were barfing, and you looked so horrible—"

"Stomach flu, I guess," Diana said breezily.

Sam shook her head. "How can you take the whole thing so lightly?"

"Look, it's no biggie."

Sam snorted loudly. "Yeah, right. If you want my advice—"

"I don't," Diana snapped.

"Here it is, anyway," Sam said. "Get some condoms and use them."

"Please, Sam, don't make me laugh,"

Diana shot back. "Who are you to give me a lecture on condoms? Are you gonna try and tell me you use them every time?"

What Sam wanted to say was, "Actually, Diana dear, I'm a virgin, so the matter hasn't come up." But she would never give Diana the satisfaction of knowing the truth.

"Diana, I promise you that every single time I have sex I use a condom," Sam said coolly. *Well, I'm telling the truth,* she added to herself.

"That's really good, Sammi," Lorell insisted, wide-eyed. "I mean, we all know that a girl from your background—or should I say *lack* of background?—has to be very careful about that sort of thing. How would you ever know who the father was?"

"If anyone here hasn't signed up yet, please do so now," a female voice called through a microphone from the other side of the huge room.

"Gee, I hate to barf and run, but you just bring that out in me," Sam said. She made a gagging noise, then turned and walked away.

Sam made her way through the throng

and finally reached the registration desk. A young woman wearing a crown was sitting behind the desk. She had long, glossy brown hair and big blue eyes. Next to her sat a middle-aged couple, both plump and both dressed as if they were going to a particularly elegant cocktail party, even though it was the middle of a Saturday afternoon.

"Hi, I'd like to register," Sam told the girl in the crown.

"Oh, gosh, that's wonderful!" said the girl, with the enthusiasm she might have shown if she had just been told she'd been named Miss America. "We're so happy to have you! I'm Scarlett Sweet, and this is Mrs. and Mr. Spangler." She nodded at the overdressed couple.

"I admire your taste in jewelry," Sam told Scarlett, taking in the tiara.

"Oh, this," Scarlett said, touching her crown. "This is from when I was named Miss Washington County Fair last month. I'm also Miss Salt Water Taffy and third runner-up to Miss Maine, among others!"

"Wow," Sam said, since she couldn't think of anything else to say.

"And we're so happy to have you," Mrs. Spangler said, reaching over to squeeze Sam's hand warmly. "Just fill this out." She shoved a form toward Sam.

"Okay," Sam agreed.

As Sam bent over the table to read the form, Scarlett caught a whiff of the perfume Sam had sprayed in her hair before leaving home.

"That's a wonderful perfume," she said admiringly. "Isn't it, Mrs. Spangler?"

The older woman leaned closer to Sam to smell the fragrance. "Yes, it's delightful," she said. "It's very light and fresh."

Sam smiled. "Thanks," she said. "It's called Sunset Magic. My friends and I helped create it."

"You actually created your own perfume?" Scarlett gasped, amazed. "Wow! I never met anyone like that before!"

Just then another girl came up to the registration desk, and Sam moved aside to let her talk to Scarlett and the Spanglers. She quickly filled in the form she'd been given, then read the fine print at the bottom. The preliminary round would be held in five days, the finals in a week. All finalists would take part in evening gown, talent, bathing suit, and interview competitions. There was an entrance fee of $150.00.

"One hundred and fifty dollars?" Sam exclaimed out loud. *"Excuse me?"*

"Major ripoff," a voice near her said.

Sam turned to see Kristy Powell, a gorgeous, flirtatious blonde who wrote a gossip column for the *Breakers*.

"Are you entering this thing?" Sam asked her.

"Not me," Kristy said. "I'm covering it for the *Breakers*."

"Why does it cost so much to enter?" Sam asked her.

Kristy laughed. "That's easy. So Mr. and Mrs. Pageant-head can make some bucks."

"I don't follow."

Kristy moved closer to Sam. "It's like this. The Spanglers are professional pageant-givers. It's a for-profit enterprise. They go all over the country doing this. Usually a local chamber of commerce will agree to cosponsor, and then they move in."

"Gee, I guess that explains why they're

so friendly," Sam murmured. "They're in it for the bucks. I had no idea."

Kristy nodded. "Pageants are big business. It's really only worth entering if you truly believe you have a shot at winning."

"Well, that's exactly what I believe," Sam said coolly.

Kristy grinned. "That's what everyone says. Which is precisely why the Spanglers can make so much money. Good luck!" She sauntered off and lost herself in the crowd.

Sam nibbled on the end of her pencil. *Should I do this?* she pondered. *Do I really want to risk so much money?* Just the week before, the Cheap Boutique, the hippest clothing store on the island, had sold another one of Sam's original designs, called Samstyles, and for the first time in her life she actually had a little money saved in her bank account.

"Oh, what the heck," she said out loud, rummaging through her purse for her checkbook. "Nothing ventured, nothing gained, and all that stuff!" She wrote out a check for $150.00 and walked back over to Scarlett.

"Here you go," Sam said, handing in her application.

"Great, uh . . ." Scarlett scanned Sam's application until she saw her name. ". . . Samantha!"

"Call me Sam."

"Sam, isn't that cute?" Scarlett said to Mrs. Spangler.

"Darling," Mrs. Spangler agreed, "and so are you. Have you ever been in a pageant before?"

"Not really," Sam admitted.

"Oh, dear," Mrs. Spangler said, looking deeply distressed. She turned to her husband.

"We'll help her along, dearest," he told his wife, patting her hand.

"Yes, we will," Mrs. Spangler said firmly, giving Sam a radiant smile. "After all, there's a first time for everyone. There was even a first time for Scarlett, right, dear?"

"Right, Mrs. Spangler," Scarlett replied dutifully.

"Well, I wasn't actually planning to make it my life's work," Sam pointed out.

Scarlett nodded as if Sam had said something profound. "I can understand that. But do you know that some girls train their whole lives in the hope of one day becoming Miss America? The pageant system is a long and honored tradition."

"Uh-huh," Sam said lamely. "That's . . . really interesting."

"You know, Sam dear," Mr. Spangler said confidentially, leaning across the table toward Sam, "no girl wins her very first pageant."

I wonder if I can reach for my check and tear it up, Sam thought, her heart sinking. "They don't?"

"Well, hardly ever," Mrs. Spangler amended.

"I won my first pageant," Scarlett said after she had given an application to a short girl with long black hair. "I have to tell you, Sam, there's nothing in the world like winning a major beauty pageant. When they put this crown on my head . . . well, it was the happiest day of my life."

"How much did you win?" Sam wondered. *In other words, let's get down to the real deal.*

"Well, my first pageant win was Miss Moonlite," Scarlett said. "I was sixteen years old. I won a thousand-dollar savings bond, a new wardrobe from a major department store, and a modeling portfolio and a modeling contract with an agency in New York."

"Wow," Sam said, impressed in spite of herself.

"Pageants are really just wonderful scholarship opportunities for young women," Scarlett said.

"And you won the very first pageant you ever entered?" Sam asked.

"I did," Scarlett affirmed.

"Why, that's true, Scarlett, you did," Mrs. Spangler said, as if she had just realized this was so.

"So, like, how did you do it?" Sam asked her eagerly.

"There's only one way," Scarlett said solemnly. "I took the seminar."

"The seminar?" Sam echoed.

"Just fill this out and bring it back!" Scarlett called gaily to the last girl in line. Then she turned back to Sam. "Yes, the seminar. It's sort of an all-day cram course in how to win a pageant, and believe me, it's worth every penny."

"How many pennies are we talking about, exactly?" Sam asked dubiously.

"It costs a hundred and fifty dollars," Scarlett admitted, "but—"

"Whoa, hold up," Sam said. "Are we talking *another* hundred and fifty dollars?"

"Yes," Scarlett said, "but—"

"That's three hundred dollars just to compete!" Sam cried.

"Look at it this way," Scarlett said. "If you win, it will all have been worth it, and if taking the seminar really helps your chances . . ." She didn't need to finish the rest of her sentence.

Sam turned to Mrs. Spangler. "And I suppose you give the seminar."

"Oh, no," Mrs. Spangler said. "A very important professional flies in to do that. He has trained more pageant winners than anyone else in the world."

"Really?" Sam asked cautiously.

"Three Miss Americas," Scarlett said reverentially.

Mr. Spangler beckoned Sam over to him with a curve of his finger. "Please understand, we don't invite just anyone to take the seminar."

"You don't?" Sam asked.

"Definitely not," Mr. Spangler said. "We tell only certain girls about it."

"The special ones," Mrs. Spangler said. "We could never possibly register all the girls who would want to be a part of it, so we must be selective."

"And you, Sam," Scarlett said, "really have something special."

Sam couldn't decide whether this was true or a scam. "You can tell by looking at me?"

"You're tall, slender, and beautiful," Mr. Spangler said, counting off on his fingers. "Do you have a talent?"

"I'm a professional dancer," Sam said with pride.

"I knew it!" Mrs. Spangler said. "You move like a dancer!" She turned to her husband. "Can we pick them or can we pick them?"

"So, when is the seminar?" Sam asked.

"Monday," Scarlett replied, then she bit her lower lip in consternation. "I hope it's not already full."

"Check for me," Sam said eagerly.

Scarlett reached for a clipboard behind her. "I think we can probably fit one more person in, but I'm not sure. . . ."

"You can," Sam said, "I'm sure you can." She quickly found her checkbook and wrote out another check, which she handed to Scarlett. "So, I'm registered now, right?"

"Right," Scarlett said. "Come back to this same room at nine o'clock Monday morning, and be prepared to stay all day. Bring flats and heels, a bathing suit, and a long gown. Oh, and a notebook for taking notes." She reached into a box behind her and pulled out two flyers, which she gave to Sam. "Read these handouts, too. They'll tell you everything you need to know about the pageant and the seminar."

"Okay, I will," Sam said, "and thanks!"

"Here," Mrs. Spangler said, lifting a large plastic button out of another box. She leaned over and pinned the button on Sam's vest. "This is only for our seminar girls!"

Sam looked down at the button. It read WE WALK IN BEAUTY: THE SEMINAR. "Nice," Sam said, even though she really thought it was tacky.

"Wear it proudly," Mrs. Spangler said.

"Thanks," Sam said. "I'll see you Monday."

Most of the girls had left the conference room, but just before Sam got out the door, she ran into Lorell and Diana again.

Her heart sank.

Both Diana and Lorell were wearing buttons that read WE WALK IN BEAUTY: THE SEMINAR.

"You?" Lorell asked incredulously.

"You?" Sam asked right back.

"I thought it was supposed to be some exclusive thing!" Diana protested.

"Gee, I thought so, too," Sam sneered. "But I guess they let anyone in."

"I'm just curious, Sammi," Lorell asked. "How long did you have to stand on your street corner making dates with boys so you'd have enough money to pay the entrance fee?"

Diana laughed. "Ooh, two points for you, Lorell."

Sam looked over at Diana. "You know, it's funny," she said. "When Lorell was off the island, I almost started to think you were human. I even thought we might actually become friends. But I guess I was wrong."

For a just a moment something like shame seemed to flicker across Diana's eyes, but it was gone as quickly as it had arrived. "I'm sure you misunderstood. Why would someone like me ever want to be friends with someone like you?" she asked snootily.

"I'm asking myself exactly the same question," Sam said with dignity. Then she turned and walked away.

THREE

"A beauty pageant?" Pres asked, looking dubious. He lifted the hair from the back of Sam's neck and tickled her lightly. "Somehow it doesn't seem like your style, girl."

It was that evening, and Sam, Pres, Emma, and Kurt Ackerman were sitting together on a blanket out by the far pier. The night was balmy, and the sun had just set. In the distance, classical music was playing from someone's tape deck.

"Winning is my style," Sam said with a shrug. "I mean, I could win a whole bunch of stuff!"

"You didn't want to enter, huh?" Kurt asked Emma.

"Oh, no," Emma said quickly. "Besides, who ever heard of a short beauty queen?"

"We could put you on stilts," Kurt teased, reaching over tenderly to brush a lock of blond hair off her face.

Sam smiled. *After what happened between the two of them, I never, ever thought I'd see them together again,* she thought. *I really thought Emma and my half-brother, Adam, were going to be a major item. But Emma never really got over Kurt, and I guess he never got over her, either.*

"Well, you know we'll all be out in the audience rooting for you," Pres told Sam with his lopsided grin.

"You think I can win?" Sam asked him.

"Shoot, girl, I *know* you can win," Pres said, leaning over to give her a loud kiss on the forehead. "That's for luck."

"Are you going to make up an original dance for the talent part?" Emma asked, drawing her knees up to her chin.

"I guess," Sam said with a sigh. *But the truth of the matter is that I'm a dancer, not a choreographer,* she admitted to herself. *Well, I'll think of something.*

"I got an interesting phone call from the Chamber of Commerce today," Kurt said casually. He took a sip of the lemonade in his paper cup. "It seems some famous people are flying in to be judges for the pageant, but the Chamber of Commerce is asking two local people to be on the panel, too, kind of to round things out."

"Do they want you to recommend someone?" Emma asked him.

"No," Kurt said. "They want me to be the someone."

"Yes, mama!" Sam whooped. "Now I've got one of the judges in my pocket!"

"Are you going to do it?" Pres asked him.

"I'm not too into the concept of beauty pageants, really," Kurt said.

"Hey, it's a scholarship program for women!" Sam objected. "What could be bad?"

"Well, that's an arguable point," Kurt said. "Anyway, I said I'd do it if the Chamber of Commerce makes a donation to COPE."

Sam knew Kurt was referring to Citizens of Positive Ethics, an organization dedicated to preserving the natural state of the island and to helping the poor year-round residents, who were often forgotten.

"And they probably told you to take a flying leap," Pres guessed, "since they could get some other dude who would be only too happy to judge pretty girls parading around in bathing suits, right?"

"Wrong," Kurt said. "I was surprised, too, but they said yes. I guess they figure it'll make them look good or something."

"So you're a judge?" Emma said stiffly.

"Don't get bummed out, Em," Sam said. "He's doing it for charity!"

Kurt nodded solemnly. "I promise to hate every minute of it."

"Liar," Emma said, but she managed to laugh when she said it.

Kurt leaned over and kissed Emma softly. "Believe me, I would not do anything that might make me lose you again."

"Me, neither," Emma whispered back fiercely.

"Uh, excuse me," Sam called out, "but if the two of you are about to play suck face, I'm outta here."

"We can wait," Kurt said lightly. "Not too long, though," he added, reaching for Emma's hand.

Look at her, Sam thought, staring fondly at her friend. *I've never seen her look so happy. I hope this time Kurt isn't so possessive and hung up about Emma's money, and I hope Emma is more honest, and I hope—*

"Who else entered this thing?" Pres asked, pulling Sam out of her reverie.

Sam groaned and threw herself back on the blanket. "The two-headed she-devil," she reported, "namely Diana and Lorell." She turned her head toward Pres. "I'm taking this pageant seminar thing on Monday—some world-famous expert is flying in to teach it—and they're in it, too. God, how disgusting."

"It's too beautiful a night to talk about Diana and Lorell," Emma said, snuggling up against Kurt.

"Want to go for a walk?" he asked her softly.

"Sure," she replied.

Kurt stood up and reached for Emma, pulling her to her feet. "We'll be back . . . eventually," Kurt said, and the two of them walked away across the sand.

43

Sam rolled onto her stomach and watched them, a happy smile on her face. "And they lived happily ever after," she said blissfully.

"Maybe so, maybe not," Pres replied.

"Cynic," Sam accused. "Come on, those two were made for each other."

Pres moved closer to Sam and began to give her a sensual back rub. "I believe they really care about each other," he agreed. "But they come from two totally different worlds. I don't know if they can ever get over that."

"Love conquers all," Sam said, closing her eyes. "Mmm, that feels unbelievably good."

"I could do it a lot better without this T-shirt," Pres pointed out, lifting the shirt from her back.

"No prob," Sam said. *My bra has flowers all over it,* she realized, *and it looks just like a bathing suit top. Actually, my bikini top is probably skimpier.* She lifted the T-shirt off and lay back down.

"Sam, Sam, Sam," Pres said appreciatively. He lifted her hair, bent over, and kissed the back of her neck. Then he slowly began kissing down her spine.

Finally she turned over and reached up for him. "I hope they don't come back for a really, really long time," she said.

They didn't.

"You're never gonna win, Sam," Allie Jacobs said bluntly as she poured some milk on her Rice Krispies.

"Never," echoed Becky.

"I bet Diana's got the inside track," Allie added.

Sam sat down at the Jacobses' breakfast table and took a contemplative sip from her mug of steaming-hot coffee. It was the next morning, Sunday, and the twins were planning an all-day picnic with their best friends, Dixie Mason and Tori Lakeland. It was Sam's day off, and Emma was supposed to call her so that they could have lunch together at the country club.

"Where's your dad?" Sam asked, ignoring the girls' jibes at her.

Allie made a face. "At the driving range."

"With Kiki!" Becky added. "He's always with Kiki." Kiki was Kiki Coors, an actress Dan Jacobs had actually met through the twins. Lately the woman had been acting a little too motherly for their liking.

"He's teaching her to play golf," Allie added significantly. "That has to be a sign of something or other."

"Can you imagine the two of them golfing together into their twilight years?" Becky gave her sister a horrified look. "You don't think he's actually going to, like, *marry* her, do you?"

"Never happen," Allie said firmly. "We'll go on a hunger strike or something."

"I thought you guys didn't think she was so bad," Sam reminded them, taking a bite of her muffin.

"She's getting worse and worse," Allie said. "Last night she told us we should discuss the movie we saw with her, because it was 'very adult' and she thought it might have upset us. I mean, give me a major break! I thought *we* were going to have to explain it to *her!*"

Sam had to laugh. *They're obnoxious,* she

46

thought, *but I've got to admit they can be really funny.*

"Anyway," Allie pointed out, "beauty pageants are always fixed, and since Diana has major bucks, she's in and you're out." She picked up that day's edition of the *Breakers* and started scanning it for Kristy's gossip column, practically the only thing in the paper she ever read.

"I don't think it's fixed," Sam said.

"What about your talent part?" Becky asked her. "What are you gonna do?"

"Dance, probably," Sam replied, choosing another muffin.

"Yeah, but what dance?" Becky asked. "You can't just stand there and shake. And you know Diana is going to sing."

"Let's face it, she really can sing."

Allie pointed to something in the paper. "Hey, does the name Christopher McGriff mean anything to you?" she asked.

Sam drew a blank. "Can't say I know who he is," she replied honestly.

"Yeah, I know," Allie said. "There've been so many guys in your life, it's hard to keep them all straight from one week to the next."

Christopher McGriff. God, that sounds familiar, but I just can't place it. Sam struggled to kick-start her memory. *I know that name. But from where?*

"Well," Allie continued, "it says here that Christopher McGriff from the Long Beach Bay Ballet Company is on the island for a few days, raising money for next season."

And then it came to Sam. *Of course!* she thought. *X! I didn't recognize his name because he calls himself X—like in Christmas—instead of Chris! I totally fell for him when he was on the island earlier this summer. He's the most gorgeous, fantastic, wonderful guy I've ever met in my life—except maybe for Pres. Wasn't I surprised when I tried to kiss him one night and he told me he was gay!*

"X!" Sam exclaimed. "He's the greatest guy! He taught you guys to dance at the country club, didn't he?"

"Yeah," Becky said. "What a babe. Hey, I just got the greatest idea! Maybe he could make up a dance for you for the beauty pageant!"

"I thought I didn't have a chance," Sam reminded her.

"Well, I might have exaggerated a little," Becky amended. "So, isn't my idea great?"

"Yeah, actually, it is," Sam said slowly. *But if X is on the island and he hasn't even called me, why would he want to help me with some beauty pageant?* she wondered. *He told me that if he ever got back here, he'd call me right away. Oh, well, people say stuff like that all the time, and—*

Brrring! The phone rang. "It's gotta be Emma for me," she said, getting up to retrieve the cordless phone from the kitchen counter. "Miss Sunset Island speaking," Sam trilled into the phone. "Sounds kinda great, dontcha think?"

It wasn't Emma. It was a male voice. "Uh, I'm sorry, I must have the wrong num—"

"No, *I'm* sorry," Sam interrupted, a little embarrassed. "This is the Jacobs residence. Sam Bridges speaking."

49

The male voice laughed heartily. "Sandi!" he said happily. "It's you! This is X."

So he really did call me, Sam thought delightedly. After she'd been introduced to X, he'd deliberately called her Sandi as a joke, even sending flowers addressed to Sandi to the Jacobses' house after he and Sam had a particularly wonderful night dancing together at the country club.

Of course, that's when I was so sure that he was straight! Sam remembered. *Was I in for a big surprise! Just goes to show you can't tell by looking.*

"Hey, big guy!" she exclaimed. "I just heard you were on the island! Too cool!"

"Is it Chris?" Becky asked eagerly.

Sam nodded.

"Invite him over," Allie hissed. "He is to die for!"

"Becky and Allie say you are to die for," Sam told X into the phone, knowing he would appreciate the joke. "They want me to invite you over."

X laughed. "They're way too young, and *definitely* not my type," he replied.

"He says you're too young, but he's flattered," Sam translated to the twins.

"That's the story of my life," Becky said with a sigh. "Come on, Allie, let's go listen to the new Pearl Jam tape." The twins left the kitchen.

"They're gone," Sam reported into the phone. "Do you think they'd flip out if they knew you were gay?"

"Sam, I always assume people will flip out unless I know differently," X said. "It makes my life much safer."

It must be terrible to have to live that way, Sam thought. "So, X, what are you doing back here, anyway?" she asked, swallowing the last bite of her muffin.

"Raising money for the ballet," X answered. "Lots of checkbooks here love me."

"Pass some of it over to me," Sam suggested, sitting back in the kitchen chair. As she and X traded small talk she recalled how, earlier in the summer, she had been ready to quit the Flirts, and quit her job with the Jacobs twins, in order to form a dance duo with X that would tour across America.

51

That wasn't the greatest idea, Sam recalled, *but we sure can dance together.*

"Listen," X said, "I'm going to be at the country club around lunchtime today. Can you join me?"

"Yeah, love to," Sam replied. "I'm meeting Emma there anyway."

"Terrific," X answered. "You can be my good-luck charms."

"For what?" Sam asked.

"Getting big donations out of the membership," X answered cheerfully. "Can't produce ballets without the checky!"

"Emma and I will give you all the good luck you could possibly need," Sam promised. "Hey, maybe she'll even make a donation to your ballet company!"

"I never ask friends," X replied.

"Well, what if she offers?" Sam asked.

"That would be a whole different ballgame," X admitted. "But I don't want you even to bring it up to her, okay?"

"Rats," Sam said. "I was hoping if I planted a little fund-raising seed in Emma's head, you'd do me a big, fat favor."

"I'd do you a big, fat favor anyway," X

said. "Anything for the coolest redhead Kansas ever produced."

Sam grinned. "Is that really what you think?"

"If I were straight, I'd propose," X said with a laugh. "What's the favor?"

"I'll tell you when I see you," Sam said. "Later, big guy!"

Sam hung up and crossed her fingers superstitiously. *If I can get X to choreograph my dance for the beauty pageant, I really, truly could win. I'd win all that incredible stuff and, best of all, I would beat Lorell Courtland and Diana De Witt. Now, what could be better than that?*

FOUR

"Look!" Sam said as she and Emma strolled into the packed main dining room of the country club. "There he is!" She pointed to X, who at that moment was holding court at the bar.

"And look who's with him!" Emma exclaimed.

"Lorell. That figures," Sam groaned. Then she turned her attention back to X. "Gay or straight," she continued, "that is one of the finest-looking guys I have ever seen in my life." He was dressed in a white silk shirt, black pleated cotton trousers, and black Italian-made boots. His shoulder-length sandy hair was swept back off his face, and he looked like he'd added even more muscle to his already perfect physique.

Sam had dressed carefully herself, as had Emma. Sam had on one of her newest Samstyles—a black velvet scarf tied sarong-style at the waist to create a miniskirt, over a white cotton slip from the thrift store that she'd covered with tiny pearl buttons. Her hair was held up in a loose ponytail with a scrap of white lace, and her ever-present red cowboy boots were on her feet. Emma had on beige wide-legged pants made of the finest Egyptian cotton, with a cream-colored T-shirt that stopped just above her waist, exposing a fraction of bare, tanned skin.

"Looks like it's Lorell's turn to fall in love with X," Emma said with a smile, checking out how Lorell was practically draping herself over X.

"Can you blame her? If only she knew!" Sam grinned. When X had been on the island earlier in the summer, it had been Diana who bragged about how she and the dancer from California were an item.

"Let's go rescue him," Emma suggested.

"Don't you dare say a word!" Sam cautioned her as the two of them walked across the crowded room.

"I would never tell Lorell he's gay," Emma said. "But—"

"Ssssh!" Sam shushed her. "I have a brilliant idea!"

Sam and Emma slowly approached X and Lorell. When X spotted the two of them, he jumped to his feet, a broad grin on his face.

"My favorite redhead!" he exclaimed, giving Sam a tight bear hug.

"I missed you!" Sam exclaimed happily.

"Hi, Emma," X added, reaching to give Emma a hug, too. "You two look wonderful!"

"You actually are friends with these two?" Lorell drawled.

"You might say that," X replied.

"Well, if you weren't so cute, I'd hold it against you," Lorell simpered, resting her hand briefly on his bicep. She looked Sam up and down. "Sammi dear, I know you are financially challenged, but you don't really have to dress in actual rags like that, do you?"

"These 'rags' happen to be my own design and they sell for a lot of money," Sam pointed out hotly.

"Do tell!" Lorell trilled, laughing as if someone had told a hilarious joke.

"Lorell was just telling me," X confided, "that she's a real patron of the arts. Isn't that right, Lorell?"

"My family has a whole wing named after us in the art museum in Atlanta," Lorell said proudly.

"Imagine," Sam pretended to marvel.

"It's true," Lorell assured her, taking a sip of the cranberry juice she'd been drinking. "And we've been giving money to the Atlanta Ballet for simply *ages!*" She touched X's arm again. "We could never give to another ballet company—I'm sure you understand. It would just be wrong, don't you think?" She leaned closer to X. "Of course, you and I could discuss it privately. . . ."

"Lorell, can I talk to you for a moment?" Sam asked her, her voice totally sincere but a twinkle of no-good in her eye.

"You?" Lorell asked dubiously.

"Why not?" Sam replied. "I don't bite."

"Well," Lorell said, standing up, "I don't see why not. Excuse me," she told X, leaning over to kiss him on the cheek. "I'll try my very best not to keep you waiting, sir."

"No problem," X replied.

Sam left Emma chatting with X. She led Lorell off to one side of the bar and lowered her voice practically to a whisper.

"I wanted to talk to you, woman to woman," Sam said confidentially.

"Well?" Lorell asked impatiently, folding her arms. She glanced over at X and Emma, who were laughing together at some joke. "Hurry up," she urged Sam. "You can't leave a guy that handsome alone for five minutes."

"I just wanted to tell you that I know he really likes you," Sam confided. "I mean, he *really* likes you. If you catch my drift."

"How do you know?" Lorell demanded.

"Oh, he might have said something about it when he was here on the island earlier this summer," Sam lied. "He might have said that he wanted to get to know you. *Bad*."

Lorell looked at Sam, trying to determine

59

whether Sam was telling the truth or not. "Why are you telling me this?"

"Because X is my friend, and I want to see him happy," Sam said earnestly. "I mean, he's obviously totally out of my league, but he's had some tragedy in his life—I can't go into it now—and he deserves some joy, don't you think?"

"That's true," Lorell agreed slowly, looking over at X. "Tragedy, huh?"

"Tragedy," Sam agreed, nodding solemnly.

"Was it too awful?" Lorell pressed. "I just have to know."

"All right," Sam said. "But you have to promise you'll never, ever tell him I told you."

"Oh, I swear!" Lorell exclaimed breathlessly.

"Well, there was this girl," Sam invented. "He was engaged to her. And she looked a lot like you!"

"Go on!" Lorell urged.

"She was in a tragic accident. They were out on a fishing boat together, and . . . he lost her."

"Lost her?"

Sam nodded. "Overboard. They think it was a shark. All they ever found was . . ." Sam's eye lit on the twinkle of Lorell's bracelet. ". . . her diamond tennis bracelet, floating by the boat."

"Oh, my word!" Lorell breathed, her hand over her heart. She looked over at X, who was deep in conversation with Emma. "And she looked like me, you said?"

"Yeah," Sam replied. "Maybe you could mend X's broken heart."

Lorell looked Sam over, and Sam used all of her acting skills to keep a straight face. Finally Lorell seemed to make a decision. "Thanks, Sam," she said slowly. "I didn't think you had it in you to be human."

"My pleasure," Sam said seriously.

Lorell touched the dainty diamond tennis bracelet that circled her narrow wrist, and she shuddered. "I'll do my best to make it up to him," she vowed dramatically.

"Oh, no doubt," Sam agreed.

"Excuse me," Lorell said, straightening out her dress and smoothing her hair. "I hear destiny calling me."

She headed straight for X.

*　　*　　*

"So, that's the deal," Sam concluded. "Will you help me?"

X had finally managed to get away from Lorell and join Emma and Sam for lunch. He was ecstatic—Lorell had given him a two-thousand-dollar donation for the ballet company. While they were eating lunch Sam had told X all about the beauty pageant and how badly she needed his help to choreograph her dance.

"Choreograph a two-minute dance for me, please," she begged X. "You do it, I win."

"What happens if I don't?" X answered, a twinkle in his eye. He took another bite of the peach cobbler he'd ordered for dessert.

"Sam makes you babysit for the twins," Emma quipped.

"Worse than that," Sam said. "I lose, big."

"There are worse things than losing," X commented.

"Not if I lose to Lorell Courtland or Diana De Witt."

"What makes you think I can do it?" X asked, finishing the peach cobbler.

"Ha! You can do it with your eyes shut!" Sam cried. "With one leg tied behind your back!"

"What kind of music do you have in mind?" X asked her.

Sam looked at Emma, who looked back at her blankly. They hadn't discussed this.

"How about one of the Flirts' songs?" Emma finally suggested. "Something really upbeat."

"Such as?" Sam mused.

"'Love Junkie'!" Emma suggested eagerly. "You already move so well to it, you know? It would be perfect!"

"Gee, Emma, you ought to manage my career," Sam said with a laugh. "'Love Junkie' is perfect! It's got a great funk beat. You could be brilliant with that tune, X!"

"I don't know. . . ." X hesitated.

"Please, please, please," Sam wheedled.

"Only if you tell me what you told Lorell that made her write that check to my ballet company," X decided.

"Okay," Sam said. "I made something up about how you had a tragic past." *Well, that's part of what I said,* she amended to herself.

"And that made her give me a donation of two thousand dollars?" X asked skeptically.

"What can I tell you? She's a drama queen!" Sam said innocently. "It appealed to her."

"You don't think she thinks I'm interested in her, do you?" X asked dryly.

"Never," Sam replied.

X raised his eyebrows at her. "Never?"

"Well, you got your donation, didn't you?" Sam pointed out. "I mean, isn't that all that matters?"

"I'm thrilled to get the donation," X admitted, "but I still have a feeling there's something you're not telling me."

"*Moi?*" Sam asked innocently.

X looked over at Emma. "Do you know what this is about?"

"No," Emma said. "I really don't."

"What's my big tragic past supposed to be, anyway?" X asked Sam.

"Oh, forget about Lorell!" Sam insisted. "She's d-u-l-l, not to mention boring. Let's talk about me and how much you love me and how you could never let me down in my moment of need."

X laughed. "I really did miss you, Sandi," he told her. "There's no one else quite like you."

"Does that mean you'll do my dance?" Sam asked hopefully.

"Sure, I'll choreograph your dance."

"Yippee!" Sam whooped, jumping up to throw her arms around X. "You won't be sorry!"

"I'll be sorry if you've gotten me tangled up with Lorell in some way," X warned.

"Never," Sam insisted innocently.

Just at that moment Lorell came out of the ladies' room and walked by their table. Sam hadn't even realized she was still there. Lorell leaned close to X and whispered in his ear, but it was loud enough for Sam to hear. "I'll call you tonight," she whispered. "I'm going to make you a very, very happy man."

She was gone before X could open his mouth.

"Sam . . ." he began.

Sam smiled weakly. "Can I help it if you're irresistible?"

From across the room they saw Lorell near the door, gazing lovingly back at X. She put her fingers to her lips, kissed them, then blew the kiss to X.

Sam started laughing so hard that she had to run to the ladies' room so she wouldn't pee in her pants.

Emma followed her.

"Oh my God, that is the funniest thing I ever saw in my entire life!" Sam gasped between peals of laughter.

"What did you tell Lorell?" Emma asked, leaning against the sink.

Sam wiped the tears from her eyes and told Emma what she'd told Lorell. "Tell me that isn't hilarious!"

"It's funny," Emma agreed. "But I don't know if X will think it's funny."

"Oh, come on," Sam said as she went into a stall and locked the door. "He just got a two-thousand-dollar donation out of her. He'll think it's hilarious!"

"I don't know," Emma said, letting herself into the next stall. "I hope you're right."

"I'm right," Sam insisted. *Hey, X got his donation, I got a choreographer, and Lorell got what she deserves,* she thought. *How could I not be right?*

FIVE

"Sam, hi!" Scarlett said at the doorway to the Sunset Inn's conference room. She hugged Sam as if she were a long-lost friend.

"Hi," Sam said, suffering through the overly enthusiastic hug. *Not that you don't seem really nice and everything,* Sam thought, *but, like, we just met.*

It was the next morning, and Sam had just arrived for the We Walk in Beauty seminar. She was dressed in faded jeans and an old Disney World T-shirt featuring Mickey and Minnie Mouse smooching. In her oversized dance bag she had two different Samstyles to choose between for the evening gown portion of the pageant, and two different itty-bitty bikinis. She'd worn her red cowboy boots, but she'd packed some heels and some flats, along with all the cosmetics she owned. She noticed that Scarlett was dressed in a white suit with super-high heels, and she was still wearing her crown.

Maybe it's superglued to her head, Sam thought with a giggle.

She scanned the room, which was already filled with thirty or so girls, all chatting at once. She saw Lorell and Diana across the room talking with Mr. and Mrs. Spangler (who were also dressed to the max), as well as some other girls she vaguely knew from around the island. *Half the girls in here aren't even good-looking,* Sam noted, her eyes sweeping across the room. *That girl near the window must wear a size sixteen at least, and the blonde sitting near the podium has zits on her zits.*

Sam turned back to Scarlett. "Uh, didn't you say that only special girls got invited to be a part of this seminar?" she asked Scarlett.

Scarlett nodded eagerly. "It's really lucky we could fit you in, isn't it?"

70

"Yeah, lucky," Sam replied dubiously. *I have a feeling they could have fit Freddy Krueger in if he'd showed up with a hundred and fifty bucks.*

She looked over at Diana and Lorell and got a sinking feeling. Diana was whispering in Lorell's ear and looking over at Sam. *I can't even stand to be around those two.*

"Hello, I'm Carrie Alden. Sorry I'm late," a familiar voice said to Scarlett. "I had to pick up a new flash at the last minute."

Sam turned around. "Girlfriend!" She cried, and gave her friend a hug. "What are you doing here?"

"The Chamber of Commerce hired me to photograph the pageant!" Carrie explained with excitement. "Isn't that fabulous? I got a call last night."

"Whoa, too cool!" Sam agreed. "They paying?"

"Yes, they're paying," Carrie said with a laugh. "Although I would have done it for free for the experience."

"You're not late," Scarlett assured Carrie. "And we're so happy to have you here!"

"Thanks," Carrie said, a bit taken aback

at Scarlett's enthusiasm. "I'll try to be as unobtrusive as possible."

"I'm sure you'll be wonderful," Scarlett said, squeezing Carrie's hand. "If you'll excuse me, I'm just going to ring Lord Owen's room and tell him we're ready to begin the seminar."

As Scarlett turned to leave Sam stopped her. "Wait a second. Did you just say Lord Owen?"

"Yes," Scarlett said. "He's the founder of We Walk in Beauty," she added in a worshipful tone.

Carrie and Sam looked at each other. When Emma and Kurt were planning to get married, Emma's mother had insisted on having a world-famous wedding consultant fly in from England. His name was Lord Owen Witherspoon—a supercilious older man who loathed everything that wasn't high society. But could it possibly be the same person?

Sam turned back to Scarlett. "Listen, this may be a dumb question, but is this Lord Owen guy British?"

"Why, yes, he is," Scarlett replied.

"Is he in his fifties, tall, kind of portly?" Carrie asked.

"I would use the term big-boned," Scarlett said gently.

"Is he also a wedding consultant?" Sam asked.

"Only for royal weddings," Scarlett said. "I mean, believe me, you can't hire someone like Lord Owen Witherspoon to do just any wedding—"

"It's him!" Sam yelled, laughter bubbling out of her. "Wait till I tell Emma!"

"You know Lord Owen?" Scarlett asked.

"He did our friend's wedding," Carrie explained. "Well, not exactly, because they never got married."

Scarlett looked confused.

"It's kind of a long story," Carrie said, biting her lip to keep from cracking up.

"Your friend must be really special, that's all I have to say," Scarlett said with a sweet smile. "Excuse me, please. I have to go ring him."

"Lord Owen!" Sam squealed. "That dude is a joke! Remember how he tried to get us to do that stupid wedding walk down the aisle? And how nasty he was to Kurt?"

"I can't wait to see him demonstrate the bathing suit strut," Carrie said with a laugh. She pulled off one of the cameras that were strung around her neck and checked the lens. "Listen, I need to go be unobtrusive and take some candids," Carrie said. "Have fun."

Sam took a seat near the back of the room, as far away from Diana and Lorell as she could get. In just a few minutes Scarlett and Lord Owen came in and marched up to the front of the room. *Yep, it's the same Lord Owen, all right,* Sam noted, taking in his perfectly coiffed silver hair and his immaculate suit. *I bet the guy can hide a good thirty pounds under a suit that well-cut,* she thought. *I can't believe I spent one hundred and fifty big ones for him!*

Mr. and Mrs. Spangler rushed over to Lord Owen, who kissed Mrs. Spangler first on the right cheek and then on the left. He shook hands with Mr. Spangler, then turned to scan the crowd of girls. His eyes flickered when he got to Sam.

I wonder if he recognizes me from Emma's wedding party, Sam thought.

"Ladies, I am proud to introduce to you the founder of We Walk in Beauty, Lord Owen Witherspoon!" Mrs. Spangler gushed.

"My dear young ladies," Lord Owen intoned, his eyes sweeping the crowd, "we are about to embark on a journey into the land of beauty, grace, and perfection. But perfection doesn't come easily. We must work, work, work to truly walk in beauty."

Sam smothered a laugh. *I remember this guy always uses the royal "we",* she recalled. *He hasn't changed a bit!*

"To wear the tiara is an honor," Lord Owen continued. "We are here to prepare the recipient of that honor for her destiny."

"You'd think someone was about to be crowned Queen of England," a girl in front of Sam hissed to her friend. Her friend just dug her elbow into the other girl's ribs.

A hand went up from the front of the room. Lorell.

"Yes?" Lord Owen asked.

"Sir, is it true that you trained three Miss Americas?" Lorell asked breathlessly.

"Yes, certainly," Lord Owen replied.

"Well, I just want to say how proud I am to be here at the We Walk in Beauty seminar with you," Lorell said respectfully.

"Of course you are," Lord Owen replied. "Now, please line up at the back of the room so that we can look you over. Up, up, up," he said, making gestures with his hands to indicate that the girls should all get up from their chairs. "Form a single line, ladies. And remember, anything we tell you is for your own good."

Sam rolled her eyes as she walked by Carrie, who was clicking away with her camera. The thirty girls stood there self-consciously while Lord Owen walked slowly back and forth in front of them, taking them in from head to toe.

"Your name would be . . . ?" Lord Owen asked a short, muscular girl wearing cut-offs and a denim shirt.

"Michelle Jenkins," the girl replied nervously.

"Miss Jenkins," Lord Owen repeated. "When one has thunder thighs, one makes the wise choice to cover them up."

76

"But I'm not fat, I'm muscular," the girl said, taken aback. "I'm a gymnast."

"We see," Lord Owen said, nodding. "However, knotty muscles are not a pretty sight unless one is on the balance beam."

"Yes, sir," the girl said in a small voice.

"What's she supposed to do for the bathing suit competition, then?" Sam asked.

"We would suggest prayer," Lord Owen said. He walked over to Sam. "You are . . . ?"

"I'm Sam Bridges," Sam said. *I guess he doesn't remember me.*

"Sam would be a nickname, we assume?" Lord Owen asked drolly.

"Short for Samantha," Sam explained.

"How butch," Lord Owen said. He narrowed his eyes, as if he was thinking hard. "Have we met before?"

Sam nodded. "You did my best friend Emma Cresswell's wedding," she reminded him. "I was in the wedding party."

Lord Owen shuddered. "The fiasco of our life," he recalled. "She planned to marry a garbage collector or something equally revolting, did she not?"

"He's a swimming instructor, and drove a taxi to earn—well, he was . . . but—"

Lord Owen held up his hand. "Please. We would prefer not to dwell on sordid memories. It wrinkles the face."

Lord Owen continued to walk down the line, offering suggestions—or insults, depending on how you looked at it.

"Well, we certainly have our work cut out for us," Lord Owen said when he reached the end of the line. "However, we appreciate a challenge. Let us begin this morning with the bathing suit walk. Ladies, please change into your bathing costumes and your heels."

"The ladies' room is across the hall," Mrs. Spangler called, "or you can use the smaller conference room next door."

Sam quickly picked up her dance bag and headed into the ladies' room, where she was able to snag a stall. *Which suit, which suit,* she mused, holding up both a hot pink fishnet bikini and a black and white polka-dot number with little frills across the bust. *Hot pink,* she decided, wriggling into the suit. *I look great in pink.*

When she came out of the stall she jock-eyed for position in front of a mirror, put on some hot pink lipstick, and tied her hair up with a hot pink scarf. *Looking fine,* she told her reflection.

"Damn, I just got mascara in my eyes," a girl said from behind her. She practically fell over Sam, it was so crowded in there.

Sam pushed through the crowd and out into the hallway, where she slipped on a pair of white high heels. *Well, I feel like a real bimbo wearing high heels and a bathing suit,* she thought. *The things I'll go through to win a car.*

"Why, Sammi, you look just perfect," Lorell purred, walking by Sam on her way back to the conference room.

Sam noticed that Lorell had on a one-piece royal-blue maillot with high-cut legs.

Sam waited a moment, knowing Lorell would add something insulting. Only she didn't. "Hold on, did you just give me an actual *compliment?*"

"Why, yes, I believe I did," Lorell said. "After all, how can we walk in beauty on the outside if we don't walk in beauty on the inside?"

"Oh, yeah, good point," Sam said.

Lorell waved her fingers at Sam and walked away. *Huh?* Sam thought. *Maybe she's being nice to me because I fixed her up with X, the love of her life. Ha!*

Sam hurried into the conference room and threw her dance bag down on a chair.

"Ladies, gather together in the corner, please!" Mrs. Spangler called over the chattering voices.

Sam joined the other girls in the back corner of the room, thinking how truly stupid everyone looked in high heels and bathing suits.

"Quiet down, ladies," Lord Owen called. Everyone immediately shut up and waited for instructions. Once again Lord Owen's eyes lit on Sam. "Miss Bridges?"

"Yes?"

"Step forward, please."

Sam stepped.

Lord Owen looked her up and down slowly. His nose twitched as if he had just smelled something bad. "Miss Bridges, what are you wearing?"

Sam looked down at herself, then back at him. "It's called a bathing suit."

"No," Lord Owen corrected, "we call it two teensy-weensy pieces of deplorably cheap fabric masquerading as a bathing suit."

"Hey, I paid a lot for this—" Sam objected.

"Miss Bridges," Lord Owen interrupted, "we have no desire to discuss price tags. But at the risk of having you actually answer the question, if you are going to wear such a garment, why should you bother to wear anything at all?"

"I happen to like this bikini," Sam said, although she could feel her face beginning to redden with embarrassment.

Lord Owen sighed. "Miss Bridges, is it safe to assume you know how to read?"

Sam crossed her arms and gave Lord Owen the evil eye. "It's safe," she snapped.

"Then what did your seminar instructions say?" Lord Owen asked.

"What instructions?" Sam wondered.

"The ones I gave you when you registered," Scarlett said. "Didn't you read them?"

Sam vaguely remembered receiving some sheets of paper that Scarlett had handed her; she'd folded them and stuck them into her purse. *But I never actually read the things!* Sam realized. "I remembered to bring everything you told me to bring," she told Scarlett.

"We refer you to number seven on the We Walk in Beauty preparation list," Lord Owen said as Mr. Spangler handed him a printed sheet of paper. "'All bathing suits should be one-piece. Bikinis are never, ever worn in a legitimate beauty pageant. It is overkill,'" Lord Owen read out loud.

Sam looked around at the other girls. Sure enough, all of them had on one-piece bathing suits. *And I was just too ditzed-out to notice,* Sam thought in chagrin. She turned back to Lord Owen. "Oops," she said meekly.

"Oops, indeed," Lord Owen agreed. "A very major oops."

From behind her Sam heard smothered laughter, and she turned around to see Lorell and Diana snickering at her expense. *So that's why Lorell told me how great I looked,* Sam realized. *The bitch.*

"Ladies, please watch as the correct form for modeling swimwear is demonstrated," Lord Owen told them.

Scarlett had slipped out of her white outfit, under which she was wearing a one-piece white bathing suit.

"One of our dearest protégées," Lord Owen said, smiling at Scarlett. "We are never wrong when we select a protégée. And our protégées almost always win. Now remember, the walk is a long stride with the feet coming to the center, making a long, narrow line, thusly," Lord Owen explained. He nodded at Scarlett and Scarlett walked.

"Excellent," Lord Owen approved. "The head is held high on the neck. Think of a string, ladies, a string up through your center and out the top of your heads, attached to the ceiling. You are tall, you are graceful, you walk in beauty."

Heads all around Sam nodded eagerly. *Big deal,* Sam thought. *It's just your basic runway-model walk without the snotty attitude.*

"Now the pivot turn," Lord Owen said.

Scarlett pivoted.

"And then you face the judges and the cameras, you smile . . ."

Scarlett gave a dazzling smile on cue.

"Do not look snotty or smug, but generous, loving, the personification of all that is beautiful. The face should say, 'I am honored that you should select me.' No smutty men's magazine licking of the lips—true beauty is of a higher nature," Lord Owen concluded. He nodded at Scarlett and applauded her, which caused the whole group to join in.

"Lovely, dear," he told her.

"Thank you, my lord," Scarlett said.

Gag me, Sam thought. *Why doesn't she just curtsy?*

"Ladies, a few general tips before you practice the walk," Lord Owen said, addressing the group. "We find that Vaseline applied to one's gums helps one deliver a truly radiant smile."

Scarlett picked up a small tube of Vaseline and squeezed a blob out onto her finger. She pulled her lips back in a grimace and quickly rubbed the Vaseline all over her gums. Then she smiled.

"Perfect," Lord Owen said. "Also, ladies, we find that glue on the inside of the seat of one's bathing suit keeps it from riding up in the most unattractive fashion."

Sam looked over at Scarlett. *Don't tell me she's going to strip and glue her butt for us right here and now!*

Scarlett merely held up a small glue stick as a prop.

Sam looked over at Carrie, who kept snapping away with her camera. "Can you believe this?" she mouthed at her friend. Carrie shrugged and kept on shooting.

Well, I can't believe it, Sam thought as Lord Owen droned on and on. *And I don't see good old Lord Owen stripping down to his bathing suit to demonstrate a pivot turn. At least it would be good for a laugh.*

"Now then, ladies, do we have a volunteer who would like to try the bathing suit walk?" Lord Owen asked.

"I will," Diana said, stepping forward.

Sam checked Diana out. She had on a white bathing suit with gold bands around the halter neck and the high-cut legs. Her chestnut curls framed her lovely features. She looked tanned, fit, and absolutely gorgeous.

"Your name?" Lord Owen asked.

"Diana De Witt," Diana replied coolly. "Of the Boston De Witts?"

Lord Owen's eyebrows shot into his hairline. "Excellent stock," he said approvingly.

"Breeding does tell, doesn't it?" Diana agreed. She looked over at Sam, taking in her tiny bikini, and then she shook her head with disgust.

"Would you care to try your walk, Miss De Witt?" Lord Owen asked.

"Of course," Diana replied. She walked across the room exactly the way Scarlett had, her head held high. Then she did a slow pivot turn, her eyes sneaking back to the front and her body following, and smiled at the imaginary judges. Then she turned again and walked back to the group.

"Bravo!" Lord Owen raved. "And that, ladies, is how it is done! Take five, please." The Englishman went over to Diana to speak with her.

Sam's heart sank. *Who am I kidding?* she said to herself. *I don't have that kind of confidence. I'm flat-chested and gawky and poor. I can't compete against Diana De Witt.*

"She's not so great," Carrie whispered in Sam's ear.

Sam turned quickly—she hadn't even realized that Carrie was standing next to her.

"She looks great, though," Sam replied glumly. "She makes me feel like five miles of bad road."

"Forget her," Carrie advised. "You are an original, you're great-looking, and you have major talent. You're going to be wonderful."

"Yeah," Sam agreed halfheartedly.

But when she looked over at Lord Owen, who was sucking up to Diana De Witt big time, she knew he had found his protégée, and it definitely wasn't her.

SIX

"Whew, I'm whupped," Sam said tiredly, flopping down on the floor of the small rehearsal studio that she had rented at Sunset Dance Concepts on Main Street.

"We're not finished yet," X told her, but he reached into his dance bag, pulled out a red plastic water bottle, and tossed it to Sam.

"You saved my life," Sam said, guzzling down the water.

"Thirsty?" X asked innocently.

"No, not in the least," Sam replied. "I can keep up with you without drinking a thing. I just didn't want you to feel bad." She tossed him back the empty water bottle.

It was late the next morning—the only time that X said he had free to choreograph a number for Sam for the Miss Sunset Island pageant. Luckily the Jacobs twins were at camp, where they were working as counselors-in-training, so she had some free time. And even though she had hoped to spend the morning relaxing before meeting Emma for an outdoor lunch on the boardwalk, she'd readily agreed to meet him.

Now she wasn't so sure. X had choreographed a number for her, yes, but it was so strenuous and full of leaps, splits, and spin moves that Sam had been totally out of breath the first time she rehearsed it.

Not that I'd admit that to him, Sam thought, wiping the sweat off her forehead with her T-shirt.

After teaching Sam the routine, X had made her practice it over and over and over, correcting her moves, her positioning, and her timing until she was ready to keel over from exhaustion. Fortunately, just as she was about to beg for mercy, X had called a break.

"So, do you like 'Love Junkie'?" Sam

asked X, flexing the sore muscles in her calves.

"I'm getting kind of sick of it, to tell you the truth," X replied, sitting down next to Sam on the floor.

"It's our best number!" Sam protested.

"Well, I guess it's okay," X conceded, "but the backup vocals are a mess—especially on the melody." Then X winked at Sam. Sam knew that he knew the backup melody line on the tape mix had been laid down by Sam herself.

"You're a pain," Sam said with a laugh, leaning her head back against the wall. She rolled her head around to loosen up her neck. "So, listen, tell me the truth. Do you think I have a shot with this?"

"Sure," X said. "You've been choreographed by the master himself." He stretched out his legs and arms as he talked, and Sam was struck once again by just how gorgeous this guy was.

And not just on the outside. He's going to make someone very happy someday, she commented to herself.

A sudden thought crossed Sam's mind.

"You're not choreographing for anyone else, are you?"

"Not unless you count Lorell," he replied.

Sam grabbed the sleeve of X's T-shirt. "You're not really—"

X threw his head back and laughed. "You're right, I'm not really. But I sure had you going!"

Sam punched X in the arm. "Creep! I believed you!"

"It's my patented sincere and innocent look," X teased. He looked over at Sam. "I still want to know what you told her about me."

"That would spoil all the fun!" Sam said with a laugh.

"Yours maybe, not mine," X said.

Sam grinned. "It's truly hilarious. I told her that—"

At that moment someone knocked on the door to the mirrored studio, and X called out loudly, "Yeah!"

In walked Lorell Courtland, smiling the biggest come-hither smile Sam had ever seen.

Well, she's really decked herself out, Sam

remarked silently, snorting back her laughter. *Check out that uni!*

Lorell was wearing a frilly baby-pink miniskirt with a matching frilly pink short jacket over a white lace camisole. In one hand she was carrying a lacy pink parasol and in the other a wicker picnic basket.

Lorell proves that even the rich can have atrocious taste, Sam thought.

"Gee, Lorell, what are you doing here?" Sam asked. She shot a glance over at X, who looked as surprised as she was.

"Hi, X, and hello, Sam," Lorell drawled, sidling over to him. She sat down next to him and spread her frilly skirt around her legs prettily. "They told me at the club you were here, so I thought I'd pop in and say hey."

"Hey," X echoed noncommittally.

"Oh, I think it's so sweet the way you said 'hey,' almost like you were really Southern!" Lorell cried. "It's sooooo cute!"

"Gee, thanks," X deadpanned. "Uh, we were just about to get back to rehearsal."

"Oh, I wouldn't want to interrupt a true *artiste* at his work," Lorell hastened to explain. "But I did want to invite you to have lunch with me. You wouldn't believe what I have in this little ol' picnic basket! Beluga caviar, strawberries, Camembert cheese, *foie gras*—"

"Gee, Lorell, that was . . . thoughtful," X said, "but we need to work some more, and then I really have to—"

Lorell cut him off with a wave of her hand. "Oh, poo!" she exclaimed. "I wanted to talk about a gift I might be able to secure for your ballet company. A large gift. *Very* large."

Sam could see a flicker of interest cross X's face.

"I appreciate it, Lorell," X said. "How about later this afternoon? I'm working now, as you can see."

"Oh, hush, I'm sure Sammi will let you go early," Lorell trilled, "seein' as how she's so understanding about why you're here, right, Sammi? I mean, you did come to the island to raise money for your ballet company, didn't you? And we are talking about a *very* large gift."

"Anything for the arts," Sam said with a

sigh. *How can I possibly expect him to stay here and work with me for free when he might get a major chunk of change out of Lorell for the ballet company?* she thought gloomily.

"Listen," Lorell said flirtatiously, "I'll meet you in, say, an hour. That'll give you time to finish up. Memorial Park, under the oak tree. I won't take no for an answer." She kissed one finger and then brought it to X's lips.

"Okay," X agreed reluctantly.

"Then ta-ta!" Lorell cooed. "I'm really looking forward to it."

"I'm sure you are," Sam mumbled under her breath as Lorell started to leave the room. Lorell turned slowly.

"Did you say something, Sammi?" Lorell said with a smile.

"Just that I'm sure you're going to have a peachy time together," Sam improvised.

"Oh, we will," Lorell said as she turned to leave the room. "We definitely will. And Sammi . . ."

"Hmm?"

"I wouldn't bother working too hard on

your little talent number if I were you," Lorell suggested confidentially. "I mean, it's not like you have an actual chance to win! Bye-bye!"

"She brought a picnic lunch right to the studio?" Emma repeated, taking a small bite of pizza. "I can't believe it."

"Believe it," Sam said. "I saw it with my own eyes." She took a huge bite of a calzone she had just purchased and looked out at the ocean reflectively as she chewed.

It was a couple of hours later. Sam and Emma had met by the boardwalk, as they'd planned. But when they'd tried to get into their favorite open-air restaurant, the place was packed with tourists and they would have had to wait at least an hour for a table to open up. So Sam had talked Emma into just buying some Italian fast food and eating it on one of the benches that faced the ocean.

"I hope X gets her to make a large donation," Emma said.

"I bet Lorell hopes the same thing, but I

doubt they're thinking about the same kind of donation!" Sam joked.

"You're terrible!" Emma cried, laughing hard.

"To know me is to love me," Sam replied, taking another huge bite of her calzone.

The two of them ate in silence for a while, looking at the waves splashing their way methodically up the beach. The tide was coming in, and families were packing up their blankets and towels and moving back up the beach, closer to the boardwalk.

Lorell's words kept running over and over in Sam's mind. *It's not like you have an actual chance to win.* She licked some cheese off her fingers and sighed. *Maybe it was totally stupid for me to have entered,* she thought. *Maybe I just blew three hundred dollars on an opportunity to make a fool out of myself in front of the entire island.*

"I refuse to think that way," Sam said out loud.

"What way?" Emma asked, wiping her fingers on her napkin.

"Nothing," Sam said, not wanting to admit to Emma how truly insecure she felt or how much money she had spent. She decided to change the subject. "So, Emma-bo-bemma, are you going to tell me about your little walk on the beach with Aquaman, or am I going to have to torture it out of you?"

Emma laughed. Aquaman was the nickname that Diana De Witt had given Kurt when he was a swimming instructor at the country club.

Emma got a dreamy look in her eyes. "It was wonderful," she reported.

"Details," Sam demanded, starting on her second calzone. "I demand details."

"We talked a lot," Emma said.

"Well, duh, as Becky would say," Sam commented.

"It's important for us to talk," Emma said softly. "We have a lot to talk about."

"I'll say," Sam quipped. "No, really, tell me."

"We both got to say we were sorry," Emma told Sam. "I mean, really sorry. It was . . . it was as if we had finally stopped blaming each other, and we could both see the mistakes we'd made, you know?"

"Wow," was all Sam could muster.

"Kurt said he was sorry that he had such a hard time dealing with me and my family's money, and I said I was sorry, too."

"You've told him that before," Sam pointed out.

"I know," Emma said. "But this time it was . . . I don't know . . . it was different. I don't know how else to explain it."

"Good for you," Sam said supportively, her voice taking on the accented tones of a German psychiatrist. "You demonstrate an acceptable level of maturity zat I most zertainly lack!"

Emma grinned.

"So, what did he say?" Sam prompted, raising her voice over the cries of a flock of seagulls flying by at boardwalk level.

"He accepted my apology," Emma murmured. "And I accepted his. From the heart. Really."

"Wow," Sam said again.

"Sam," Emma declared quietly, hugging herself, "I am so happy."

"Because . . . ?"

"Because I thought I'd lost him forever,"

Emma said quietly. "And I was wrong." Tears of happiness filled her eyes.

"You were wrong," Sam said, echoing her friend's words, and marveled to herself about how things rarely turn out the way you think they will.

"He talked to his dad about us," Emma went on. "Kurt says even his father is beginning to understand that not everything was my fault—that's a major breakthrough."

"You really think Kurt can learn not to be so possessive," Sam asked, "and to chill out about your being rich?"

"I do," Emma said firmly. "I believe it with all my heart." She looked earnestly into Sam's eyes. "Sometimes people really do change, Sam. If they want to badly enough."

"I am truly happy for you, Em," Sam said, reaching over to touch her friend's hand. "I mean it."

Emma's only reply was the sweetest, happiest smile that Sam had ever seen.

Eight hours later, Sam was sitting around the kitchen table of the Jacobses' house

100

with Carrie, Becky and Allie Jacobs, and the twins' friend Dixie Mason.

The day before, at the seminar, Lord Owen had made a point of telling the contestants to practice for the interview portion of the competition. So Sam, who had to stay home with the twins that night anyway, had invited Emma and Carrie to come over to help her. Emma had to stay with the Hewitt kids, but Carrie had come.

"Major brainstorm from my brilliant brain!" Becky had cried. "I'll invite Dixie over! Her older sister is Miss Mississippi and is competing in the Miss America pageant!"

"And Dixie was America's Little Miss Sweetheart!" Allie had added. Then she'd clapped her hand over her mouth. "Oops, she doesn't want anyone to know that. Her days as a beauty-pageant contestant are over."

"Thanks, but I'm not sure Dixie can help me much," Sam had replied. She was skeptical that a kid like Dixie could do anything for her.

"Sam, Dixie is going to be an astronaut,"

Allie had reported. "She's smarter than all of us put together."

As it turned out, Allie was a hundred percent on target. Dixie not only knew about the ins and outs of pageants, but she had turned into the impromptu leader of the evening practice session. Sam and Carrie both looked with awe at the tiny blond bundle of Mississippi energy sitting at the head of the kitchen table.

"So Sam," Dixie drawled, "what would your answer be if the judge asked you the following question?"

"I don't know," Sam replied.

"Ah haven't asked the question yet," Dixie reminded her.

"Okay, ask away," Sam said breezily.

"Samantha Bridges," Dixie recited in a masculine-sounding voice, "who is the woman in history you most admire, and why? Begin your response in twenty seconds. The rest of y'all can make up answers, too."

Sam thought quickly, feeling the pressure. Carrie, Allie, and Becky all looked deep in thought as well.

"Time's up," Dixie said, looking up from her wristwatch. "Contestant?" She looked directly at Sam.

"Uh, the most admirable woman in history is my friend Carrie Alden," Sam improvised, "because she always has good judgment and is a good friend."

"Wrong," Dixie said flatly. "That answer will not do. Does someone have a better idea?"

"Cindy Crawford," Allie suggested.

"Never pick someone better-looking than you are," Dixie advised.

"Hillary Clinton?" Becky suggested.

"Way too controversial," Dixie said quickly. "The judges could be Republicans!"

"How about Marie Curie?" Carrie suggested, putting down the glass of iced tea she'd been holding. "She won a Nobel Prize for her work on radioactivity—"

"Which eventually led to the creation of the atomic bomb," Dixie finished. "Out of the question."

"How about someone from the Bible—maybe Sarah, Abraham's wife?" Becky asked, rolling her eyes. "I mean, we don't

103

know if she was a babe or not and she had no political party affiliation."

"Won't go," Dixie answered matter-of-factly. "Never pick a person who's famous because she's someone's wife. The judges hate that. They want *you* to want to be a wife one day, but you're not supposed to pick someone because her husband was famous. Get it?"

"No," Becky said bluntly.

"So," Sam said—a little exasperated, and also a little embarrassed that a thirteen-year-old girl was running the show, and doing it so effectively—"what's an acceptable answer?"

"There is only one surefire, four-star-acceptable answer," Dixie replied.

"What's that?" Becky asked.

"Mother Teresa," Dixie said, as if she were giving the answer to the question of what two plus two equals. "Because she has accomplished so much in the interest of mankind, and has served the poor self-lessly."

"But that's ridiculous!" Sam exclaimed.

"Mother Teresa is ridiculous?" Carrie asked Sam.

"No, she's not ridiculous," Sam countered. "But the whole idea that there's, like, a perfect answer is ridiculous. I mean, it doesn't have anything to do with what I think or feel at all. *Anyone* could give that answer."

"Sam," Dixie said in a calm voice, "do you want to be Miss Sunset Island?"

"Yeah," Sam replied reluctantly.

"Good," Dixie said. "So if you are asked this question at the pageant, how will you answer?"

Sam felt everyone's eyes on her.

"Mother Teresa," Sam replied in a monotone, "because she has accomplished so much in the interest of mankind, and because she has served the poor selflessly."

Everyone at the table applauded.

"Pretty good," Dixie Mason said, "but not perfect."

"Not perfect?" Sam asked, astonished. "But I repeated just what you said."

"You didn't say it with passion and conviction," Dixie pointed out.

"You're kidding," Sam said.

Dixie shook her head.

Sam stood up and put her hand over her heart. "I most admire Mother Teresa," she said passionately, "because she has accomplished so much in the interest of mankind, and because she has served the poor selfishly . . . shoot, I mean selflessly!"

"A mistake like that can cost you the pageant," Dixie pointed out.

"I had no idea it was such hard work," Sam said, flopping back into her chair. "This is all just nuts. I don't think it's worth it."

"Just remember, Sam," Becky said, "I bet Diana De Witt is practicing right this minute. I bet she's got it down to a science."

"I can't stand the thought of losing to her," Sam seethed, her eyes narrowing.

"Well, you're going to unless you get this stuff right," Allie huffed.

"Hey, I'm in Dixie's hands," Sam said, reaching for a cookie.

But deep down inside, she wished she had never decided to compete in the beauty pageant in the first place. *Because deep down inside,* Sam admitted to herself, *I really don't believe I can compete with Diana.*

And I'm probably a total fool even to try.

SEVEN

"Yum," Sam said softly as Pres kissed her gently right on the corner of her mouth, sending shivers of delight up and down her spine. She turned her head slightly and returned the kiss.

"Whew," Pres whispered quietly when the kiss finally was over. "You been takin' kissin' lessons?"

"Just from a certain Tennessee musician," Sam said impishly.

"Have I ever heard of him?" Pres joked.

"Hard to say," Sam replied. "He doesn't talk much. He seems to find other uses for his lips." She leaned over and kissed him again.

It was the next morning, and Pres had invited Sam to the beach for a picnic breakfast. It was the only time that they were both free, since Sam was scheduled to rehearse with X that afternoon and then hang with the twins that night.

Normally, Sam thought, sniffing the delicious aroma of Pres's neck, *I'm not much of a morning person. But for Pres, I'll make a big exception.*

It had turned out to be a wonderful idea. Allie and Becky had gotten a ride to camp early to rehearse for some kind of skit they were in, and Pres had picked Sam up on his motorcycle just as soon as the twins had left. Now, Sam and Pres were on the beach—it was still uncrowded at this early hour—and the Maine morning had dawned clear and perfect.

"So, big guy," Sam murmured in Pres's ear, over the sound of the crashing waves thirty yards away, "I've got an important question to ask you."

"Anything," Pres murmured back.

"Anything?" Sam asked.

"You name it, it's yours," Pres said.

"It's kind of kinky," Sam warned.

"I'm a kinky kind of guy," Pres assured her.

"You're sure you're ready?" Sam asked.

"Hit me with your best shot," Pres said, pulling Sam even closer.

"All right," Sam whispered huskily in Pres's ear. "Here it is. Who is the woman in history you most admire, and why? Begin your response in twenty seconds."

"What?" Pres sat up on the beach blanket and laughed heartily.

"Who is the woman in history you most admire, and why?" Sam repeated. "Begin your response in twenty seconds."

"Uh, have you been out in the sun too long, girl?"

"Now you have only fifteen seconds," Sam pointed out, looking at her watch.

"Okay," Pres said slowly, apparently deciding to play along with whatever it was Sam was up to. "How about Jane Austen? She showed the world that women can write fiction just as well as men. Shoot, better than most men, for that matter."

"You lose," Sam said simply.

"What?" Pres asked. "What do I lose?"

"Miss Sunset Island," Sam said breezily, reaching over for one of the bagels Pres had brought. "It's too bad, really. I can imagine how cute you would have looked parading around in high heels." She peered critically at his legs. "A razor might have been necessary, of course. Too hairy, know what I mean?"

"I hardly ever know what you mean," Pres replied, taking a nibble of Sam's bagel.

"I shall explain, O ignorant one," Sam said loftily. Then she told Pres about the night before, when Dixie had asked Sam the same question in preparation for the interview portion of the contest.

"The prelims are tomorrow," Sam reminded him.

"They ask you stuff like that in the prelims?" Pres wondered.

"Nah, they don't ask you anything in the prelims. You just parade around with this plastic grin on your face while they tear you apart limb from limb."

"Sounds awful," Pres said.

Sam shrugged. "Women are judged on their body parts all the time," she said. "At least this time the winner actually gets something for it. Anyway, Dixie says that the interview question can make or break the contest, so I'm practicing early. Frankly, your answer stunk."

"What was wrong with it? I love Jane Austen," Pres challenged good-naturedly, putting down the container of orange juice he'd been drinking from.

"Writers are too obscure," Sam explained. "What if the judges have never heard of Jane Austen? They'll feel like you're trying to be superior to them. Who was she, anyway?"

Pres laughed. "Remind me to give you one of her books sometime."

"I probably won't read it," Sam said honestly. "Anyway, ask me the same question I asked you."

"Are you serious?"

"Go for it. Pretend you're a pageant judge."

Pres picked up a big spiral-shaped seashell that was next to their blanket and held it as if it were a microphone. "Miss Bridges," he said in a suave voice, "can you tell me, and the millions of people watching on television the world over, who is the woman in history you most admire, and why? Joan Jett is not a satisfactory answer."

Sam laughed, as Pres had recently introduced her to the music of this early '80s black-clad rebel rocker who was still cutting fabulous records. Then she composed herself, cleared her throat, and answered.

"The person in history I most admire is Mother Teresa, because she has accomplished so much in the interest of mankind and has served the poor selflessly," Sam said in a passionate and sincere voice.

Pres's jaw dropped. "Dang, girl," was all he could muster.

"Hey," Sam said simply, taking another bite of her bagel. "I've got this pageant stuff down pat."

Yeah, right, she revised to herself. *Actually, I'm scared to death. Not that I'm not going to win, but that Diana De Witt is going to place higher than I will.*

"Actually," Pres replied, "you're nervous as hell about it."

This time, it was Sam's jaw's turn to drop.

"How did you know?" Sam asked quietly.

"I know you," Pres answered. "Am I right?"

"Yup," Sam managed.

"Maybe this will help build up your confidence," Pres offered. He leaned over and gave Sam another delicious kiss.

"Well, I loved the kiss, but it doesn't help my confidence. You could spend the next nine, ten hours telling me how fabulous I am," Sam suggested. "That might help. Better yet, bribe a few judges for me!"

"You won't need to resort to that," Pres assured her. "Mother Teresa, huh?"

"Mother Teresa's the winning answer," Sam echoed affirmatively. "I'll kiss to that."

"Love! Love junkie, baby!"

The song ended, and Sam jumped as high as she could into the air, her loose red hair flying way up above her head, and then came down to the floor with her legs in a perfect split.

"Yeah!" X called, and snapped off the tape deck. "You've got it!"

"I do?" Sam asked, still in the split on the floor.

X tossed her a white towel. Sam caught it as she stood up, and mopped at her sweat-soaked forehead.

"You do," X confirmed. "Now you're going to have to do it without sweat flying off your face onto the judges' pristine tuxedos. It's so tacky to sweat on a judge."

"Sure thing, master," Sam said, breathing hard.

It was that afternoon, and Sam and X were spending their final two hours of rehearsal at Sunset Dance Concepts. X had drilled Sam relentlessly on his choreography, and only on the last three repetitions had Sam completed the entire routine without X stopping to correct her form or execution.

"You do it like that," X said seriously, walking over to Sam and handing her the plastic water bottle, "you've got a chance of winning."

"The talent portion, anyway," Sam said,

taking the water bottle and squirting a stream onto her face and neck. "Hey, who's the most admirable person in history, and why?"

"Mother Teresa," X answered without skipping a beat, taking Sam by the arm and leading her over to a couple of chairs near the mirrored far wall of the studio. "Because she has done so much work in the interest of mankind and done it selflessly."

Sam stopped and looked at X in shock. "How'd you know that?" she demanded.

X smiled. "I was a judge at the Miss Long Beach Bay pageant this year," he explained. "They always try to get someone from the arts community."

"And that was—"

"You got it," X said to her, taking her by the elbow again. "That was the question in the interview portion of the finals."

"Wait, I don't get it," Sam said, patting her face with the towel. "If everyone knows the question and every pageant-head knows the answer, what's the point of asking it?"

"Got me," X replied. "Maybe to separate

those in the know from those innocents who really think it's all up to chance."

The two of them sat down together. "How's your fundraising going?" Sam asked him, reaching over to towel off her neck. She was wearing a black leotard with the stomach cut out, red leggings, and black high-top aerobic shoes. Her body was completely soaked with sweat from X's intense training.

"Incredible," X said seriously. "This island is going to support the first part of my season this fall."

"Has Lorell given you a lot?" Sam asked innocently.

X gave Sam a dirty look. "What is up with her, can you tell me that?"

"How should I know?" Sam asked.

"Hey, the last time I saw you, you were going to tell me what you told her," X reminded Sam.

"Did she give you any more money for your company?" Sam asked.

"Yeah," X admitted, flexing one of his calves. "She threw me another thousand, and then she made me an incredible offer."

"Well, that's good, isn't it?" Sam asked. She deliberately didn't ask X what Lorell's incredible offer was. Knowing Lorell, it probably had lots of unpleasant strings attached.

"Of course it's good," X replied. "But she can't keep her hands off me. I obviously haven't given her any reason to think I'm interested. Which leads me to think that maybe you did."

"Who, me?"

"Sam," X warned. "Don't pull that innocent stuff on me. I know you better than that."

"Yeah," Sam admitted.

"So out with it."

"There's something about Lorell you should know," Sam began, shifting in the chair uncomfortably.

"I already know more about Lorell than I want to know, thank you very much," X said with a laugh.

"This is different," Sam said. "You know that she and Diana are my worst nightmare."

"Uh-huh," X said.

"So, I was really interested in getting Lorell to give a lot of money to your company," Sam improvised.

"Is that it?" X asked.

"No, not really," Sam answered. "I might have told her that you were interested in her."

"That is already pretty obvious," X said. "What else? Besides this big tragic past I'm supposed to have, that is."

"Okay, I'm busted," Sam said. Then she told X everything.

"She thinks the love of my life looked just like her and got eaten by a shark?" X asked incredulously.

"Something like that," Sam admitted.

"That's why she did it," X said, as much to himself as to Sam.

"Did what?"

"Told me that there'd be a check for ten thousand dollars waiting for me in Miami Beach," X explained. "If . . ."

"If what?" Sam pressed.

"If I'd go on a weeklong cruise with her at the end of the summer."

"You're kidding," Sam said.

"I couldn't make that up," X retorted.

"Are you going?"

"Believe it or not, Sam, I can't be bought," X replied. "I said I was busy at the end of the summer."

"Would you have said yes if she were a cute guy?" Sam wondered.

X gave Sam a serious look. "Like I said, Sam, I can't be bought."

"God, why do all my friends have so much integrity?" Sam grumbled.

"You do, too," X told her, leaning back against the wall. "You just don't like to admit it."

"Are you mad at me?" Sam asked.

"Not really," X said. "But I don't think you should have done it."

"I'm sorry, for what it's worth."

X stood up. "No, you're not," he said.

Sam looked up at him. "I guess you're right. I'm not. I despise her and it was a great trick to play on her."

"Nonetheless," X said, walking away from Sam, "you must be punished."

"What are you talking about?" Sam asked him, bewildered.

X strolled over to the tape deck and pushed the play button. The sounds of "Love Junkie" filled the studio.

"Get to it!" he commanded.

What can I do? Sam thought. She pulled herself to her feet and, for the umpteenth time that afternoon, launched into her dance routine.

I know it's for my own good, Sam said to herself as she drove into the opening stages of X's amazing choreography. *I only hope my legs don't go on strike!*

"Jacobs residence," Sam said automatically, picking up the ringing phone. "Sam Bridges speaking."

"Hi, Sam," a familiar voice said. "It's Carrie."

"Hey, *compadre,*" Sam replied breezily. "What's up?"

It was fairly late that evening—around ten o'clock. The twins were in the family room, playing some new video game Dan had bought them that afternoon. For once, they were out of Sam's hair. Which was good, because Sam was nervous.

Very nervous, in fact. She'd spent most of the evening in her room, thinking about the fact that the prelims for Miss Sunset Island were the next day. She'd obsessed over what to wear, smiled at herself in her mirror from every angle, then obsessed some more over whether or not she was getting a zit on her chin.

"I just called to wish you luck tomorrow," Carrie said warmly. "Break a leg and all that."

"Oh, I don't need any luck," Sam said breezily, plopping herself down on her bed.

"You're feeling confident, huh?" Carrie asked.

Sam sighed. *Who am I fooling?* she thought. *If I can't tell Carrie the truth, who can I tell?*

"Sam, you there?"

"Yeah, I'm here," Sam said. "Listen, Car, I have a confession to make."

"I'm listening," Carrie said.

"I, Samantha Bridges, do not feel confident at all. My confidence is zip. *Nada.* Zero."

"You're nervous," Carrie said.

"No sugar, Sherlock," Sam agreed. "Do you think I was a total idiot to enter this thing?"

"Not at all," Carrie insisted. "I think you could win."

"Are you just saying that because you're my best friend and I'd kill you if you didn't?" Sam asked.

"No," Carrie replied. "I'm saying it because I believe it."

"I'll love you forever for that," Sam said, "even if you're lying through your teeth." She stared up at the ceiling. "It's just that when I think about Diana up there—you know how perfect Diana is—"

"She is far from perfect," Carrie pointed out. "And you're a much better dancer than she is."

"Well, I heard through the grapevine that she's singing for the talent portion," Sam reported. "She can really sing."

"She's okay," Carrie said. "Not that great."

Sam rolled over and cradled the phone. "Sometimes . . . I know this is stupid . . . but when I get around girls with money, I just feel like this dumb, poor hick from Kansas, you know?"

"I know," Carrie said.

"Like who do I think I am, trying to compete with rich girls who go to snooty colleges?" Sam continued. "I mean, I come from a totally different world than they do."

"That's right," Carrie agreed. "You know how to milk a cow. You had a pet pig—"

"Don't rag on my porker!" Sam warned.

"I'm not," Carrie said with a laugh. "I'm pointing out to you that your background is wonderful and unique in its own way. You can't be them and they can't be you."

"Yeah," Sam said faintly, "I guess that's right."

"Listen, Sam, I'm just telling you the truth. You can't go out there with the idea that you're competing against Diana—"

"Even if I am," Sam interrupted.

"You have to go out there with the idea that you're going to do the very best you can do," Carrie said. "You have to compete with yourself, see what I mean?"

"If I were competing only with myself, I

could come in dead last and win at the same time," Sam joked.

"You know what I mean," Carrie said.

"I guess it's just that I don't want to be humiliated," Sam admitted in a low voice. "But if I get knocked out in the prelims tomorrow, I'll really feel like a failure."

"You could never be a failure," Carrie insisted loyally. "And I know you're going to be great tomorrow."

"For real?" Sam asked.

"For real," Carrie said firmly.

"Thanks, Car, you're the greatest."

"Right back atcha, Sam," Carrie said warmly. "I'll be rooting for you. Every step of the way."

EIGHT

"Ladies and gentlemen, I want to thank you all for attending the preliminary judging for the very first Miss Sunset Island Pageant," Mrs. Spangler said gaily into the microphone. "I believe I speak for the entire island as well as the pageant community when I say we hope this becomes an annual event here on your glorious island."

Mr. Spangler, who was standing next to Mrs. Spangler, applauded enthusiastically, nodding to the audience to indicate that they all should join in.

Sam could see all of this from her spot with the other eighty or so contestants, who were sitting on chairs just to the left of the podium. She picked nervously at the cuticle on her pinky and scanned the crowd. Carrie was in the back of the conference room snapping photos, but other than that none of Sam's friends were around.

Good, Sam thought. *I told them not to come to the preliminaries. Today is just the day they weed us down to the actual twenty-five girls who get to compete in the contest. If I don't make the first cut, I don't want to be totally humiliated in front of all my friends. Besides, all we do is parade around. The talent portion and all that doesn't come until the real pageant, in two days.*

"If I make it that far," Sam mumbled to herself, superstitiously crossing her fingers for luck.

"We would now like to introduce you to our distinguished panel of judges for this preliminary round," Mr. Spangler was saying.

Blah, blah, blah, Sam thought. *Other than Kurt, they're all locals I haven't got any pull with at all. The big judges don't come in until the actual pageant.*

Instead of listening to Mr. Spangler, Sam

let her eyes sweep across the girls waiting to compete. Some clearly weren't beauty pageant material. Many were borderline. *And then there are a few total knockouts,* Sam worried, feeling more and more nervous by the second. *Like that girl in the second row with the gorgeous long brown hair and the huge blue eyes,* she thought, her gaze resting on a tall beauty who looked totally self-composed. *Who is she and why have I let her live this long?*

"And finally our head judge," Mr. Spangler was concluding, "a man who is to pageants what Ronald Reagan was to presidents, Lord Owen Witherspoon!"

Sam's head snapped around. *What? Lord Owen is the head judge? He never told us that! Oh, that is just ducky. I'll be out of this contest before I even get to compete!*

Lord Owen stood up and waved his hand as if he were royalty, then sat back down. Sam saw Diana send a radiant smile to Lord Owen, who nodded back at her. Sam sank lower in her chair. *Just great,* she thought. *Just fabulous.*

"And now our parade of lovely ladies,"

Mrs. Spangler said. "Please hold your applause until the end."

The girls all got up, Sam included, and began to snake their way to the stage. Each girl had been told to dress in a way that showed off both her figure and her "true personality," as Lord Owen had put it. After trying on everything in her closet, Sam had decided on a full black skirt embroidered with cowgirls on horseback, her black-on-black vest, and her red cowboy boots for good luck. Other girls had dressed in everything from jumpsuits to dresses that looked frighteningly like they belonged on a bridesmaid at a really tacky wedding.

Lorell was up next. Each contestant was supposed to introduce herself and then tell about her interests and her career plans.

Sam took in Lorell's outfit, a perfectly tailored designer suit in red raw silk with brass buttons. *She looks like a rich flight attendant,* Sam thought, amused.

"Hey there," Lorell was saying into the microphone. "My name is Lorell Courtland and I'm nineteen years old. And I just want to say how proud I am to be here! My

130

interests are horseback riding and the arts. My dream is one day to be the best wife and mother I can be. Thank you!" Lorell waved maniacally to the crowd.

A group of people in the audience cheered and whistled. This happened after many of the contestants spoke, even though the spectators had been asked not to applaud.

Great, Sam thought. *I didn't want anyone to come, so I'll be greeted by a big, fat wall of silence. And Carrie can't very well cheer—she's the official photographer.*

The line moved forward until Sam was on the lip of the stage. *This is where they start watching me,* Sam realized. *This is where I have to shine.* She could feel a line of sweat trickling down her spine, but she vowed to ignore it. She put a smile on her face and threw her shoulders back. *I can do this,* she told herself. *I'm just as good as any of them.*

"Hello, I'm Diana De Witt," Diana was saying at the front of the stage. "I'm nineteen years old. My interests are aerobic dance and volunteer work with underprivileged children. I plan to become a talk show host so that I can reach out and affect many lives. Thank you!"

Gag me, Sam thought. *What volunteer work has Diana ever done in her life?*

Now Sam was only three girls away from the mike. Her breathing was fast and shallow. *No fainting,* she told herself. *This is not a big deal. You've been onstage lots of times. All you have to do is sparkle.*

The girl in front of Sam finished her little speech, and Sam moved up to the microphone. *It's now or never,* she told herself. *I can do this!*

She grinned into the audience, giving a special smile to the row of judges. "Hi! My name is Samantha Bridges—call me Sam," she said, hoping she sounded both confident and sincere. "I'm nineteen years old. I'm interested in just about everything, but I especially love to sing, dance, and work with kids. I also design my own fashions. I hope to become a professional entertainer. Thank you!"

"Go, Sam!" someone yelled out from the crowd. Sam turned in the direction of the voice and saw the twins standing in the back of the room. *I can't believe they came,* Sam thought, truly touched.

She sat back down and tried to wipe the sweat unobtrusively off her forehead. She did her best to relax as she listened to the last few girls do their introductions. Most didn't impress her. But the gorgeous brunette, Tawny Lynn Mayfair, looked stunning in a simple but elegant cream-colored linen shift. She did her introduction in both English and American Sign Language, saying that her dream was to work with deaf children like her little sister, Angela.

Major brownie points for her, Sam thought as Tawny walked regally from the stage.

The very last girl was a blonde Sam hadn't noticed before. She had her hair up in a ponytail and she wore white shorts, sneakers, and a white T-shirt. "Hello out there!" she called perkily. "My name is Lisa Traymoore. I'm twenty-one years old and a senior American Studies major at Colby College right here in beautiful Maine! My dream is to work with the Special Olympics, where I'm already the college assistant to the state coordinator! Thanks and God bless!"

Sam sighed, but tried not to let her dismay show. *No matter what Carrie told me, I don't see how I can compete with these girls,* she thought dejectedly. *But please, let me at least make it through this round so I won't be totally and completely humiliated. At least give me a chance to do my dance routine and show them I really am some-body.*

"And now while our judges pick the twenty-five girls who will compete for the title of Miss Sunset Island, please welcome the baton twirling of . . . Scarlett!"

A baton twirler who goes by one name? Gimme a break! Sam thought, trying not to let what she really felt show on her face in case any of the judges were looking at her.

Scarlett scampered up onto the make-shift stage in a red, white, and blue spangled leotard. From the speakers boomed a full orchestral arrangement of "Yankee Doodle Dandy." Scarlett was a whirlwind, dancing, prancing, throwing the baton up in the air over and over, catching it between her legs, behind her back, and even while doing a cartwheel. Sam was impressed in spite of herself.

There was enthusiastic applause when Scarlett finished. She posed prettily for the photographers—Sam saw Carrie right down in front snapping away. Finally Scarlett waved and hopped off the stage.

"And now, ladies and gentlemen, the moment we've all been waiting for," Mrs. Spangler said. "I have here the names of the twenty-five girls who will be competing for the title of Miss Sunset Island. I just want to say how truly lovely all eighty girls are. I'd say they're the prettiest prelims we've ever seen, wouldn't you?" she asked her husband.

"I sure would," he agreed right on cue, sticking his face in front of the microphone.

"If I call your name, please come up onstage," Mrs. Spangler said. "The names are in no particular order. Melanie Cooper, Celeste Whitley, Amber Anne Southers, Lorell Courtland . . ."

Lorell, Sam thought with disgust. *God, if she made it and I didn't, I will just die.*

". . . Nancy Finklestein, Sara Pomeroy, Lisa Traymoore . . ." Mrs. Spangler continued. When a girl's name was called she usually squealed or clapped her hands to her mouth with happiness, then ran up onto the stage.

Jeez, Sam thought, *I'm not even gonna make it through the preliminaries.*

". . . Tawny Lynn Mayfair, Kimberly Sasser, Diana De Witt . . ."

Now Sam's hands were clammy with sweat. *Okay, I can handle this,* she told herself. *I will hold my head high when I leave here. They never even got to see my talent, so what gives them the right to judge me?*

"Rebecca Feld, Annie Lee Keifer, and Samantha Bridges," Mrs. Spangler finished.

"Yeah, Sam!" both twins screamed from somewhere in the audience.

"Oh my God, that's me!" Sam said out loud, jumping out of her seat.

"Congrats," the girl next to her managed to say, even though her own face looked crestfallen.

Sam hurried up to the stage and joined the twenty-four girls whose names had been called before hers.

"Ladies and gentlemen, I present to you the twenty-five girls who will compete to be your Miss Sunset Island!"

The whole audience applauded and whistled. All the girls on stage grinned broadly. Including Sam. And it wasn't difficult at all.

"You were fabulous!" Carrie told her, hugging her hard.

Everyone was milling around. The girls who had been chosen for the finals had each been presented with a rose, but you could pick them out anyway by the happiness spread across their faces. The fifty-five also-rans left fairly quickly.

"I was, wasn't I?" Sam agreed with a laugh. "Hey, you really helped me." She craned her neck to survey the room. "Did you know the monsters are here?"

"Sam, Sam, too cool!" Becky called, running over to her. She threw her arms around her and hugged her hard.

"You made the first cut!" Allie added happily.

"How did you guys get out of camp?" Sam asked them.

"Easy," Becky said. "We just left."

"But you can't do that!" Sam protested. "It's a job!"

"Oh, chill out, Sam," Becky said. "It's lunch and naptime for the little kids. We'll be back before anyone knows we're missing."

"So how did you get here?" Sam asked. "Please don't tell me you stole someone's car and drove yourselves."

"Kiki," Becky admitted in a low voice. "She's back there somewhere."

"That was really nice of her," Sam said.

Allie shrugged. "Don't spread it around. So, look, we gotta motor. But you were pretty good up there!"

"So far!" Sam agreed happily.

"We've got a lot of work to do on you, though," Becky added thoughtfully. "You've got some serious competition from that blonde in the ponytail and the brunette—"

"Tawny Lynn," Allie put in. "She's a total fox, and she's smart. Watch out for her."

"And then there's Diana," Becky said. "She could take the whole enchilada. Which is why you'd better be prepared to work your booty off, okay?"

"Yes, Sarge," Sam said, giving her a salute.

Becky leaned close. "You might also think about investing in what nature forgot."

"What are you talking about?" Sam asked.

"Falsies, of course," Becky explained with exasperation. "We checked it out. Just about every girl competing has major hooters."

"Oh, well then, let me run out and have some quick surgery," Sam said dryly.

"That's not what the judges are going to look at," Carrie insisted, aiming her camera at a family group across the room. "Besides, Sam's dance routine is going to wow them all, right?"

"Right," Sam agreed. "I hope."

"Hope doesn't mean squat," Allie said.

"We're talking blood, sweat, and tears. The way I figure it, Dixie is our secret weapon. Okay, we're outta here. See ya later." She and Becky took off.

"Those two amaze me," Sam said, watching them leave.

"They really care about you, you know," Carrie said, slipping a new roll of film into one of her cameras.

"I generally find that hard to believe," Sam replied.

"Well, Sam, congratulations," Diana said, sauntering over to Sam and Carrie.

"Gee, thanks," Sam said sarcastically. "You know how much your encouragement means to me."

"I hear that dancer who's dating Lorell choreographed your routine," Diana said conversationally.

Sam held back a laugh. "Don't he and Lorell make a lovely couple, though?"

"I guess he took pity on you or something," Diana said, tossing her curls.

Sam shrugged. "There's just no accounting for taste, huh, Diana?"

Diana's lip curled in a nasty sneer. "Just

don't think for a moment that you're really going to get anywhere in this contest, Sam. I could beat you with my eyes closed."

"I guess you're just still feeling bad because you got kicked out of the Flirts," Sam decided. "No need to be such a poor loser, Diana!"

"You're the loser," Diana spat. She leaned close to Sam. "I'd watch my butt if I were you, stork-girl."

"Stork-girl?" Sam repeated with a laugh. She turned to Carrie. "She just called me stork-girl. I really think she's losing her touch!"

"Ah, there you are," Lord Owen boomed, coming over to Diana. He put his arm around her shoulders. "You were quite lovely up there, my dear."

"Why, thank you, Lord Owen," Diana said. "That means everything to me, coming from you."

Lord Owen turned to Sam. "Our regrets, young lady, but not everyone can make it past the preliminaries."

"What are you talking about?" Sam said. "I got picked."

"You did?" Lord Owen asked, aghast.

Sam put her hands on her hips. "Yeah, I did. Just now. You were there. You were one of the judges."

"So we were," Lord Owen agreed. "How could we make such an unfortunate error as to forget that you were chosen?" he asked dryly.

"Got me," Sam said in a cold voice.

"Excuse us," Lord Owen said, leading Diana off.

"This stupid thing is fixed!" Sam cried to Carrie. "How can the head judge walk around with his arm draped over one of the contestants?"

"It's because they start all over in the finals," Carrie explained. "In other words, right now all twenty-five of you are even again. The judges have to follow that."

"Bull," Sam snorted. "He hates me and loves De Bitch."

"Well, he's only one judge," Carrie reminded Sam.

"Do you think she's sleeping with him?" Sam asked.

Carrie looked over at Diana and Lord

Owen, who were talking with a group of people that included the Spanglers and some press people. "I wouldn't put it past her."

"Yuck," Sam said. "Serious yuck." She turned to Carrie. "Would you sleep with a guy to get something you wanted?"

"Of course not," Carrie said, snapping off a shot of Sam.

"How about for a million dollars?" Sam asked.

"Sam, you know the answer to that," Carrie said as she switched cameras.

"Yeah, yeah, you have integrity and all that." She looked over at Diana again. "The problem is, Diana never heard of integrity. I wouldn't put it past her to seduce every single judge."

At that moment Diana went up to Kurt and threw her arms around him. Sam's heart leaped into her mouth. "Look at that," she told Carrie, who turned to see Diana hanging all over Kurt.

Sam remembered how Diana had seduced Kurt the summer before, and how it had broken Emma's heart. "You don't think

Kurt would . . . ?" she asked tentatively.

"No," Carrie said firmly. "Now that he and Emma are back together, he would never do anything to jeopardize that."

But as Carrie and Sam watched Diana with her arms around Kurt, they noticed that Kurt didn't appear to move away at all.

NINE

"I just want you to know that I'm proud to be spending my last night as a mere mortal with the two of you, my dearest friends, kiss-kiss," Sam declared to Carrie and Emma, then made smacking noises with her lips.

It was the night before the pageant, and the three of them had managed to get away from both work and guys to spend a few hours together. On a whim they had purchased some sparklers on the boardwalk, and now they were sitting out on the beach near the far pier, watching the sun set.

"Are you nervous?" Emma asked Sam, letting a handful of sand wash through her fingers.

"Never," Sam said quickly. Then she

looked over at Carrie, who knew the truth. "Okay, I'm a big, fat liar. I'm nervous. Real." Sam rolled over onto her stomach and picked at a loose thread in the old quilt they were lying on. "Kurt will vote for me, won't he?"

"I don't know," Emma replied honestly.

"What do you mean, you don't know?" Sam demanded. "He's my bud, he *has* to vote for me!"

"You can't expect Emma to read Kurt's mind," Carrie pointed out. She opened the cooler they had brought with them and took out a Diet Coke.

"Sure I can," Sam said. "Now that the two of you are 'as one,'" she added.

"If you mean 'as one' in having sex, we aren't," Emma said.

"Well, I for one am shocked," Sam mocked. "I mean, how can you keep your hands off each other after waiting so long?"

Emma drew her knees up to her chin. "I don't have any illusion that Kurt and I are going to have some kind of fairy-tale relationship—too much has happened between us for that."

"Uh-huh," Sam agreed. A picture of Diana with her arms snaked around Kurt's neck flew into Sam's mind.

"We have to be smarter this time," Emma said firmly. "And smarter definitely does not involve rushing into bed."

"Or sand, or pool," Sam added, "depending on where you decide to do the wild thing. Do you think it's really possible to do it in a pool?"

Emma laughed. "Cool down, Sam. You're getting overheated."

Sam reached for a Coke, pulled the tab, and took a long drink. "So, you and Kurt are cool, huh?"

"It's wonderful," Emma sighed happily.

Sam traded looks with Carrie, then made a decision. "Em, I'm only telling you what I'm about to tell you because I love you. . . ."

"What?" Emma asked.

"Well, the other day at the prelims, Diana and Kurt were talking. . . ."

"That's not very scandalous," Emma pointed out.

"Diana put her arms around Kurt's

147

neck," Sam continued slowly, "and, well . . . Kurt just stood there. Like he . . . uh . . . liked it."

"That can't be true," Emma said.

"It is," Sam insisted. She turned to Carrie. "Tell her."

"Look, it probably wasn't what it looked like," Carrie said, sounding uncomfortable.

"You saw it, too?" Emma asked.

Carrie nodded grudgingly. "But, really, we were across the room. We don't know what was going on. And you know Diana. . . ."

"I know what it *looked* like," Sam insisted. "It didn't look good."

Emma thought a moment. "I just don't believe it was anything. I trust him. We've been through so much—"

"We probably shouldn't even have said anything," Carrie said quickly, giving Sam a pointed look.

"Maybe she was just confessing her great love for Lord Owen," Sam said. "I bet that's it. The two of them are going to run away together."

"Can you believe your wedding consul-

tant is the big beauty pageant expert?"
Carrie asked Emma, happy to change the
subject.

"Amazing," Emma said. She reached for
one of the sparklers. "Who has a match?"

"I think I have some," Sam said. She
fished a book of matches out of the back
pocket of her jeans. She struck one and lit
Emma's sparkler. "Ooh, red, my fave," she
said as she watched the glowing trails of
sparks.

"Emma loves Kurt," Emma said aloud as
she wrote with the sparkler.

Sam lit a green sparkler; Carrie got a
silver one. They all got up and ran around
the beach, making streaks of light against
the rapidly darkening sky. Finally they all
fell on the quilt again, staring up at the
stars.

"Hey, look! A shooting star!" Sam cried,
pointing to the sky.

"Make a wish," Carrie commanded.

Sam shut her eyes tight. *I wish I would
win Miss Sunset Island,* she said to herself.
I wish I'd get to see my birth father, Michael

Blady, again. I wish Pres would love me forever. I wish—

"Hey, Sam, how many wishes are you making?" Carrie asked with a laugh.

Sam opened her eyes. "One to a customer?"

"Those are the rules," Emma agreed.

"Okay, then I'm switching," Sam decided, closing her eyes again. *I wish Carrie and Emma would be my best friends for my whole life.*

"What did you wish?" Emma asked softly, looking up into the starry night.

"I can't tell you," Sam replied, her hands under her head. "Don't you wish this summer would never end?"

"Is that what you wished?" Carrie asked.

"I just said I can't tell," Sam reminded her. "This one is an out-loud-let's-discuss-it wish." She turned her head to look at Carrie. "I don't ever want the fall to come."

"Sometimes I don't, either," Carrie agreed, her eyes still fixed on the sky. "But sometimes I think that if it were the fall, I could be with Billy—"

"Instead of going back to Yale?" Emma asked, surprised.

"Would it be completely crazy?" Carrie asked. "Don't answer that—I already know the answer." They all gazed silently at the sky for a few moments. "I just miss him so much," Carrie whispered. "It's like the island has lost its magic for me."

Sam reached for Carrie's hand. *I should have been a really good friend and wished for Billy to come back,* she realized. *If only it were a wish I could make come true.*

"You guys want something cold to drink?" Carrie asked as the three girls walked into the Templetons' house a couple of hours later. Graham and Claudia had the kids with them for an overnight in Boston, so the girls had the house all to themselves.

"Got lemonade?" Sam asked, opening the cupboard where she knew the junk food was kept. "Chips, Doritos, or pretzels?"

"I'm not hungry," Emma said, getting some glasses from the cupboard.

"You eat like a bird, Emma," Sam said,

taking out both the chips and the Doritos. "Let's go out to the pool, huh?"

They took their glasses of lemonade and went out the sliding glass doors to the gorgeous swimming pool at the back of the mansion. Carrie flipped on the underwater amber light, which cast a warm glow over their faces.

"How about a swim?" Sam suggested.

"I didn't bring a suit," Emma said.

"You could borrow one of mine if you want," Carrie said. "I mean, it'll be huge on you, but—"

"God, Carrie, you aren't that big," Sam said. "You really have a complex."

"Thank you, Shrink Sam," Carrie said. "I'll just stare in the mirror and say self-affirming things, like 'You are perfect exactly as you are.' How's that?"

"A good start," Sam agreed. "Anyway, no one is here but us, so let's go skinny-dipping!" Sam pulled her T-shirt over her head and quickly dropped her jeans. "Ah, naked and free!" she cried. Then she took a running jump into the pool. "Woo!" She came up for air and splashed some water at her friends. "Come on, you guys," she coaxed them. "How often do we get to swim naked in the pool of a famous rock star?"

Emma looked at Carrie. "Actually, she's right." She unbuttoned her white blouse and slipped out of her shorts.

"Underwear, too," Sam called to her.

"What the heck," Emma mumbled. She pulled off her French lace underwear and jumped into the pool.

"You only live once—I think," Carrie said, and she, too, undressed and dove in.

"This is so great!" Sam yelled. "I love it! I'm never wearing a bathing suit again!"

"Yeah, try parading around in your birth-day suit during the pageant tomorrow, see how far it gets you," Carrie reminded her.

"Hey, Diana would do that if it meant she'd win," Sam said with a laugh. She turned over to float on her back. "Fellow foxes, this is *definitely* the life."

"Anybody home?" a male voice called.

"Who the heck is that?" Sam shrieked.

"Hello!" the voice called. "Is anyone here?"

"That voice sounds familiar," Emma said.

Carrie stood stock-still in the shallow water. "It sounds like . . . but it can't be!"

"Hey, is anyone out back?" the voice called. "Damn, no one's here."

"I'm here!" Carrie yelled quickly. "In the pool!"

"Oh, great," Sam said. "Now whoever this dude is, he's going to catch the three of us totally—"

But Carrie wasn't listening. She had jumped out of the pool and was running toward the figure that had just come around the corner of the house.

"Billy!" she screamed, throwing her arms around him. "Oh, Billy!" She was laughing and crying at the same time. "You're here! You're really here!"

Billy held Carrie tight, oblivious to the water dripping all over him. "Carrie," he said huskily, his eyes closed. "God, I missed you so much." He opened his eyes and looked down at her. "Do you want a robe?"

Carrie looked down at herself and it seemed as if only at that moment did she realize she was totally naked. "Oh, no! Let me run in and get a robe." She took a couple of steps and then looked back at him. "You're really here?"

"I am," he replied.

"Don't move," Carrie commanded, and she disappeared into the house.

"Uh, Billy," Sam said, "we're really happy to see you, too, but speaking for myself, I would shrink to nothing inside this pool rather than get out naked and throw my arms around you."

Billy laughed. "I'll go into the den. It's so good to see you guys!"

Emma and Sam scrambled out of the pool and managed to get their clothes on over their wet bodies. By the time they went into the family room, Carrie and Billy were kissing passionately.

"Come up for air so we can hug him, too!" Sam demanded. She ran into Billy's arms, as did Emma, and they hugged him fiercely.

"It's terrific to see you!" Emma told him. "We all missed you so much!"

"I missed you guys more than I can say," Billy replied huskily. He put his arms back

155

around Carrie. "And you . . . you most of all."

"Why didn't you call and tell me you were coming back?" Carrie asked him.

He took her hand and they sat on the leather couch. "I wanted to surprise you."

"Is your dad okay?" Carrie asked.

"He's better," he said. "He still needs a lot of physical therapy, but he's in good hands." Billy looked down at his own strong, square hands. "I might have to go back . . . I don't know yet."

"Oh, Billy," Carrie sighed.

"But I had to come back to you, to everyone, at least for a while," Billy said.

"My heart was breaking every day you were gone," Carrie whispered, tears in her eyes.

"I know, babe," Billy said, drawing her close.

"I love happy endings," Sam said, sniffling back some tears. "Hey, do the guys know you're back?"

Billy shook his head. "I came here first."

"We have to call and tell them!" Emma cried. "Pres will be so happy!"

"I'll call," Sam offered, racing over to pick up the cordless phone on the desk. She quickly punched in the number of the Flirts' house.

"Wuz up?" Jake Fisher, the drummer, answered.

"Hi, Jake, it's Sam," Sam said.

"How's it going?" Jake asked.

"Fabulously, actually," Sam said. "Is Pres there?"

"Yeah," Jake said. "He's back in the music room writing a tune with Jay. You want me to have him call you when he's done?"

"Believe me when I tell you this is worth interrupting him for," Sam assured him.

"Okay, I'll get him. Hold on," Jake said.

Sam could hear Jake calling to Pres, who quickly got on the phone.

"Hey, sweet thang," Pres said. "I was just thinking about you."

"Writing me a love song?" Sam asked.

"Could be," Pres agreed. "What's up?"

"I'm over at Carrie's and I have someone here who wants to talk to you," Sam said. She handed the phone to Billy.

"Hey, man," Billy said. Sam, Emma, and

Carrie watched his face. "Yeah, it's really me. I'm really back."

"Tell them to come over!" Sam hissed. "We need to celebrate."

Billy looked over at Carrie. "It's okay," Carrie said. "I'll have you all to myself afterward."

"You guys come on over," Billy told Pres. "Yeah, in a few." He clicked off the phone. "They're on their way."

"Would you mind if I invited Kurt over, too?" Emma asked shyly.

"Of course she doesn't mind!" Sam replied for Carrie.

"Call him," Carrie said with a grin.

Emma leaped for the phone. "He's coming," she said happily when she'd hung up after talking to Kurt.

"Oh, this is too wonderful!" Sam said, dancing around the room. "We need music!" She ran over to Graham's CD player and put on an Arrested Development CD, then she and Emma went into the kitchen to get some food and drinks ready, and to give Billy and Carrie some time alone.

It was only a few minutes later that Pres, Jake, and Jay Bailey, their keyboard player, showed up. Everyone hugged Billy. Sam turned the music up, and the party came to life. Ten minutes after that, Kurt showed up, too.

"This is unbelievable," Sam cried. "It's like old times, only better!"

"Will Claudia mind that you had all of us over?" Emma asked Carrie.

"She'll understand," Carrie replied, holding tightly to Billy. "It's a truly special occasion."

The music changed to a slow tune. Billy took Carrie into his arms, Kurt wrapped himself around Emma, and Sam melted up against Pres.

"That leaves you and me," Jake told Jay. "I'm dating Erin, otherwise you know I'd dance with you, big guy."

"One of these days I'm going to get a girlfriend," Jay said with a sigh.

Sam closed her eyes and leaned against Pres's muscular chest. "I'm so happy," she murmured. "Aren't you?"

Pres looked over at his best friend, Billy,

then back down at Sam. And Sam saw the tears of happiness in the corners of his eyes.

He didn't need to say a thing.

TEN

"Before we meet our lovely ladies, it is my pleasure to introduce you to our esteemed panel of judges," Mr. Spangler boomed into the microphone.

"Good luck," Lisa Traymoore whispered to Sam.

"You, too," Sam said, a little surprised. She hadn't said more than two words to the American Studies major from Colby College.

"Good luck," Lisa was saying to the girl behind her.

She must be bucking for Miss Congeniality or something, Sam decided.

She took a deep breath and tried to steady her nerves. She straightened out her skirt—the same one she'd worn for the preliminaries—and hoped that people couldn't tell she was sweating.

There must be three hundred people in here, Sam thought nervously, looking out at the crowd. All the contestants were sitting in folding chairs just to the right of the stage. From where she was she could see the faces of excited friends and relatives, craning their necks to get a peek at whomever they were rooting for.

There's my cheering section, Sam thought happily when her eyes lit on her friends in a middle row. *Becky and Allie with their best friends, Dixie and Tori. Emma, Erin Kane, Molly Mason, Darcy Laken, Pres, Jay, Jake, and Billy. Billy! I still can't believe he's really here. Oh, there's X! Too cool! I thought he'd already left the island.*

She looked around for Carrie, who was crouched in front of the stage taking photos of Mr. Spangler as he introduced the judges. He had already introduced Kurt, Lord Owen, and the owner of the Cheap Boutique.

"The honorable mayor of Sunset Island, Mr. Gamble Pinchley!" Mr. Spangler said, and the mayor stood up and acknowledged the crowd.

"And from Hollywood, please welcome the star of *Bondage Babes* and *Nanny with a Knife,* Miss Fallon Mitchell!"

Please, Sam thought as Fallon Mitchell stood up and waved to the crowd, *a third-rate actress who makes cheesy horror movies? That was the best they could do for a judge?*

"And finally, from the world of dance, a man who has choreographed three Broadway hits and is the winner of two Tony awards, Mr. Clayton Benzer!"

A very, very old man tried to get up but stumbled. Fallon Mitchell had to steady him. Even when he got up he couldn't exactly straighten out. He waved, which seemed to exhaust him, and then fell back into his chair.

He choreographed on Broadway long before I was born, Sam thought. *I hope he can still see well enough to appreciate my moves.*

"Let's have a round of applause for our panel of judges," Mr. Spangler called.

163

Breathe deeply, Sam told herself. She tried to calm her nerves by looking around the room. The back of the conference room had been draped with a red, white, and blue banner that read MISS SUNSET ISLAND PAGEANT and underneath that a smaller sign that read THE CHAMBER OF COMMERCE OF SUNSET ISLAND WELCOMES YOU AND YOUR FAMILY.

And your money, Sam thought cynically. *Without money, you are in serious trouble on this island. Which is one of the reasons I would love to win this stupid contest.*

"I'm so nervous," Lisa confessed to Sam with a tremulous smile. "Are you?"

"What's another beauty pageant?" Sam said blithely. *Well, I don't have to admit to her how nervous I am,* Sam rationalized.

"And now, ladies and gentlemen, it is my pleasure to introduce you to the twenty-five lovely contestants in the first annual Miss Sunset Island Pageant!" Mr. Spangler exclaimed.

The girls all got up, and one by one snaked their way to the stage.

So far, so good, Sam thought. *This part is exactly like the prelims. It's a piece of cake.*

All too soon it was Sam's turn at the mike. "Hello out there!" she called gaily. "I'm Samantha Bridges—call me Sam. I'm nineteen years old and I sing and dance with a band right here on Sunset Island called the Flirts. I hope to become a professional dancer. Thanks!"

Sam's friends jumped to their feet, whooping and hollering for her. She grinned as she made her way offstage and behind the blue curtain, where she had to change quickly for the bathing suit competition.

"Someone stole my heels!" a short redhead screamed.

"Look under the dressing table," a harried assistant called to her.

"Oh, no, I just got my period," another girl wailed. "I can't believe it—and my bathing suit is white!"

Sam tried to ignore everyone and concentrate on changing into her bathing suit and heels. She'd brought a one-piece suit in the same hot-pink color as her bikini. It had a halter neck and high-cut legs. The middle was cut out in the back and around the sides, and it was all held together by narrow strips of pink fabric with elastic underneath that stretched high across her hips.

I figure if you haven't got hooters, distract them with flesh, Sam thought as she slipped into her formerly white high heels—the twins had spray-dyed them hot pink the night before.

She managed to weave her way through the crowd to a spot closer to the mirror, where she fluffed up her hair and blotted her shiny face with a powder puff. She slipped some silver earrings through her ears, took a deep breath, and headed back out for the bathing suit competition.

". . . and next is Lorell Courtland," Mrs. Spangler was saying. "Lorell is five-feet, five-inches tall, and she has black hair and blue eyes. She keeps fit by playing volleyball on the beach and chasing after her darling niece, Muffy Sue Courtland, who is currently America's Little Miss Sweetheart!"

Lorell rolled her eyes, as if to say that Muffy Sue was quite a handful, and a few people chuckled good-naturedly as she made her way off the stage.

A few more girls modeled their bathing suits. Sam tried to look at them objectively. *Not fabulous, not dog meat,* she decided.

Then Lisa Traymoore was up. She wore a red, white, and blue striped suit, and she looked terrific.

"Lisa Traymoore is five-feet, seven-inches tall," Mrs. Spangler was saying. "She has blond hair and blue eyes. She keeps fit on the varsity women's hockey team at Colby College and on the intercollegiate dance drill team, which performs across the country raising money for various charities!"

Huge applause followed Lisa's turn on the stage, and Sam's spirits sank. *Okay, so Lisa is perfect so far,* she thought. *Maybe she doesn't really have any talent. I hope.*

"Diana De Witt is five-feet, six-inches tall," Mrs. Spangler said. "She has chestnut hair and blue eyes. She keeps fit by taking long walks on the sandy beaches of Sunset Island, usually accompanied by one of the many little girls who look up to her as a surrogate big sister."

Surrogate big sister? Sam thought scornfully. *That girl lies through her teeth. But I have to admit, she looks spectacular in a bathing suit.*

Diana posed radiantly in front of the row of judges, filling out her white and gold bathing suit to perfection.

Die, Sam thought. *Die right this minute.*

Two more girls took their turns, and then Sam was on the stage. She took a deep breath and stood up extra straight, grinning out at the crowd for all she was worth.

"Sam Bridges is five-feet, ten-inches," Mrs. Spangler said. "She has red hair and blue eyes. She stays fit by dancing—with her friends, with her boyfriend, even alone. Sam just loves to dance!"

She turned slowly so the judges could look at her from behind, then she looked over her shoulder and pivoted, just as Lord Owen had taught in his seminar.

Just at that moment she felt something snap at her hip. Without stopping to think, she reached down and felt the fabric, which was just about to rip. She held the fabric in place and continued to smile. Then she felt the same snap on the other side, and she grabbed that material, too.

I can't believe this is happening to me, Sam thought in a panic, though she kept the same huge smile on her face. *If I drop my hands, my bathing suit is going to fall off. I've got to do something!*

She threw her head back, keeping her hands on her hips, and tried to make it look as if she were just posing in an original way. Then she made her way off the stage.

She heard her friends screaming and yelling for her again, but she barely noticed as she ran backstage. When she peeled down her bathing suit, she saw that the elastic at her hips had actually snapped, and the pink material had frayed so much that only a few threads were holding the suit together.

But how can that be? Sam wondered. *This suit is brand-new!* She looked more closely at the elastic, and her jaw dropped open.

"Someone cut this," she said out loud. It

was clear that the elastic hadn't broken—it had actually been cut almost all the way through, and had then snapped completely while Sam was wearing the suit. And without the elastic, the pink material that covered it wasn't strong enough to keep the top and bottom of the suit joined.

"Hurry, girls, hurry," an assistant called. "Numbers one through twelve should be out waiting for the talent portion!"

"Diana," Sam said under her breath, her heart beating fast. "Diana did this to me."

"Hello, Sam," Diana said, walking by at just that moment. "Do you have a problem?"

"You did this," Sam seethed.

"Did what?" Diana asked innocently.

"You cut the elastic in my bathing suit. I know you did it."

"Sam, paranoia is not a pretty quality," Diana chided. "Excuse me, I have to go sing my little heart out."

Sam just stood there, so livid she could hardly move.

"Girls in the second group, you should be

changing into your talent outfits now!" the assistant called out, running past Sam.

"Oh, miss," Sam called out.

"Yes?" the young woman asked impatiently.

"Someone cut the elastic in my bathing suit," Sam explained. "It almost fell off me while I was out there."

The woman looked hastily at Sam's bathing suit. "I'm sure no one actually cut it."

"Yes, someone did," Sam insisted. "And I know who it was."

"Do you have proof of this?" the woman asked. "Because you are making a very serious allegation."

"No," Sam admitted, "but—"

"I'm sorry, I don't have time for this now," the assistant interrupted. "I have twenty-five girls to think of. If you want to take this up with the Spanglers later on, that's totally up to you." And she hurried off.

She didn't believe me, Sam realized. *But I know Diana did it.*

She forced herself to move. *I can't dwell on that now,* she told herself. *I've got to keep*

171

going. But I'm triple-checking everything I put on. Diana will not get away with this.

Sam pulled off what was left of her bathing suit and dressed in her dance outfit—a silver fringed leotard and silver tights. She tied her hair back with a silver ribbon. Then she checked every single seam three times before hurrying out to wait for her turn onstage.

"Please welcome Diana De Witt!" Mrs. Spangler was saying. "She will sing 'The Greatest Love of All.'"

There was a smattering of applause, and Diana confidently took the stage. She was wearing a simple white chiffon dress that hugged her rib cage and then flared out, ending just above her knees. She sang to a prerecorded instrumental track, handling the microphone like a pro.

Sam looked on with disgust while Diana sang.

She would *pick that song,* Sam thought darkly. *It's about falling in love with yourself. She sounds great, though, which just proves that there is absolutely no justice in this world.*

Diana got a huge ovation when she finished singing, which made Sam even more angry.

She watched a few more girls—a tap dancer, a pianist, and a really awful accordion player—and then Lorell was up.

As far as I know, her only talent is being rich, Sam thought, curious to see what Lorell would do.

"Lorell Courtland, reciting a poem she wrote herself, followed by her own dance interpretation," Mrs. Spangler said by way of introduction.

Lorell took the stage. She was wearing a violet chiffon skirt over a white leotard, and she began to recite.

Who cares for the little children?
I do.
Who cares for the beasts of burden?
I do.
Who sees every little bird that falls?
I do.
Who always watches over all?
I do.
Deep in your heart you must believe

I'm part of you, you're part of me.
And who will love you endlessly?
I do.

Flute music began to play, over which could be heard Lorell's prerecorded voice again reciting the same lines. Now Lorell fluttered across the stage, first becoming a child, then a beast of burden, then a little bird. Finally she twirled around, her hands fluttering as if she were in a really bad production of *Swan Lake,* and fell gracefully to the stage.

There was a moment of silence, which Sam could only suppose was collective shock, followed by unenthusiastic applause.

Lorell jumped up and took a graceful bow, then fluttered off the stage.

I wouldn't have believed it if I hadn't seen it with my own eyes, Sam marveled. *I only wish I had a videotape for posterity.*

"Next up is Miss Tawny Lynn Mayfair," Mrs. Spangler said. "She will sing 'Beauty and the Beast' from the popular movie—

and now Broadway show—of the same name!"

Tawny took the stage, looking incredible in a royal-blue silk dress that flowed around her body. She sang well, with a lot of emotion, although she wasn't as good a singer as Diana.

She probably did great in the bathing suit competition, though, Sam thought. *I must have missed her during my bathing suit fiasco.*

Sam's heart beat faster when she realized there was only one more contestant before her. She reached down to slip on her jazz shoes, and her hand happened to brush across the bottom.

It felt sticky.

Sam quickly tore off the shoes and touched the bottom of one. Her fingers came away sticky. She smelled it.

"Lip gloss!" Sam whispered fiercely. "Someone put lip gloss all over the bottom of my shoes!"

Lisa Traymoore, who was sitting next to her, looked shocked. "Are you sure?" she whispered.

"Yes, I'm sure," Sam said. "I can't wear these—I won't be able to dance at all. And I'm up next!"

The girl onstage was coming to the end of her number on the clarinet.

"What size are you?" Lisa asked quickly.

"A ten," Sam admitted, ready to cry. "I am so screwed."

"Here," Lisa said, pulling off her own jazz shoes. "They're a nine, but see if they fit."

"But I couldn't—"

"You can give them back to me right after," Lisa said. "Hurry!"

Sam quickly put on Lisa's shoes. They were tight, but she could just manage to squeeze her feet into them. "I don't know how to thank you—" she began. But an assistant was motioning frantically to Sam that it was time for her to be waiting in the wings, so she got up and hurried into place.

"Next is Sam Bridges, dancing to a song written by Billy Sampson and Pres Travis of Flirting With Danger, 'Love Junkie'!" Mrs. Spangler said.

From the audience came applause and whistles, but Sam didn't really hear them.

All her concentration was on what she was about to do.

Diana can't stop me, Sam told herself fiercely. *This is my moment.*

And she ran out onto the stage.

ELEVEN

Sam hit her final split, breathing hard. Her hands went up in the air on the button, then down under her chin in the final pose.

There was a beat of silence, and for a split second Sam thought it was just like what had happened with Lorell. *They hated me,* she thought. *Oh, no, they really hated me.*

But then the room exploded into wild applause, whoops, and whistles of appreciation. Sam jumped up and took a bow, a huge grin spread across her face. Then she waved to the audience and ran offstage.

"Oh my God, I'm a hit!" she cried out loud, jumping up and down. "I did it!" Just then she remembered that Lisa would be going on right after the girl who was now gyrating inside a Hula-Hoop, and she hurried over to return Lisa's shoes.

"Listen, I can't thank you enough," Sam whispered to Lisa.

"You were great," Lisa whispered back. "You can really dance."

"Good luck," Sam told her, then she sped away to change into her evening gown.

"How did it go, Sammi?" Lorell asked as Sam flew by her backstage. Diana was right next to Lorell. They both sat in front of the long mirror repairing their makeup. Both had already changed into their evening gowns. Lorell's gown was violet satin with a matching violet satin cape lined in pale pink. Diana wore gold lamé, strapless and slit all the way up one leg.

"I was brilliant," Sam replied evenly. "Too bad you missed it."

Diana looked down at Sam's bare feet. "Did you dance like that?"

"You would have liked that, wouldn't you?" Sam said. "I mean, you did your best to ruin everything for me."

"You really have a problem, Big Red,"

Diana scoffed. "Get some help or something."

Sam's hands clenched into fists, and she wanted nothing more than to deck Diana. But she forced herself to breathe more slowly, to calm down. *I'm not going to let her get to me,* Sam vowed. *She and Lorell have tried their best to ruin everything, but I'm not going to let it happen!*

Sam turned on her heel and walked away, working her way through the frenetic crowd of girls until she reached her assigned spot. She quickly peeled off her leotard and tights, and pulled the silver ribbon out of her hair. Then she reached into the makeshift locker that held the Samstyles gown she'd chosen to wear— black velvet wrapped to create a slim sheath, dotted with rhinestone pins scattered over the material.

The gown was gone.

It can't be, Sam thought unbelievingly, willing her heartbeat to slow down.

She looked again, searching everywhere.

No gown.

Diana and Lorell.

Oblivious to the fact that she was wearing only her underwear, Sam stomped over to Lorell and Diana. From the stage she could hear Mrs. Spangler introducing a special number by the infamous baton-twirling Scarlett.

"Give it back," Sam said in a low menacing voice.

"Give what back?" Lorell asked in exasperation.

"You know very well what," Sam snapped. "My evening gown. You took it and I want it back. Now."

Lorell sprayed her wrists lightly with designer perfume. "Sammi, honey, I have absolutely no idea what you're talking about."

Sam grabbed the back of Lorell's gown and pulled until Lorell was choking and spluttering. "I mean it, Lorell."

"What the hell do you think you're doing?" Diana yelled, slapping at Sam's arm.

Sam reached out and swatted Diana. "I swear to God, Diana, I will choke her to death if you two don't return my gown right now."

"What is going on here?" a curly-haired assistant cried, running over to them. "Get your hands off that girl!"

"But—" Sam began.

"Now!" the assistant yelled. "Or you will be disqualified from this competition!"

Sam dropped her hand reluctantly. "Look, these two girls have been trying to ruin me!"

"Ruin her?" Lorell cried. "She just tried to kill me! Y'all are witnesses!"

"They cut my bathing suit, they put lip gloss on my jazz shoes, they stole my evening gown—"

The assistant held up one hand to stop Sam. "Look, Miss Bridges, I have no idea if what you're saying is true or not—"

"It's not!" Lorell cried, rubbing her reddened neck. "She's just a stupid jealous cow!"

"—but you have no right to attack another girl in this pageant," the assistant said sharply. "Now, get ready for the evening gown competition. If you bother these girls again, you are out of here. Have I made myself clear?"

"Crystal," Sam snapped back. "But now that they stole my evening gown, what am I supposed to change into?"

"It was suggested in the literature that you bring a backup gown in case a seam popped or an accident happened," the assistant explained in measured tones. "Now, why don't you just change into that?"

Sam gave one last look to Diana and Lorell, then turned and forced herself to walk away. *Yeah, I read the stupid literature,* Sam thought. *I even brought something else—which I was so certain I wouldn't need, I left it in the bottom of my bag. I'm sure right now it's a crumpled mess.*

From the stage Sam could hear Scarlett finishing her baton number. The audience applauded enthusiastically. Now there was only a song to be sung by the current Miss Maine before the evening gown competition.

Sam ran, heading for her extra gown to see what she could salvage. As she rounded the corner she practically collided with Tawny Lynn Mayfair, who looked nothing less than perfect in a Grecian-style draped white gown.

Tawny Lynn had a large dance bag in her hand. She quickly pushed it behind her back and turned bright red. "Watch where you're going," she said in a cold voice.

"Sorry," Sam said, hurrying over to her stuff. *Jeez, this pageant stuff brings out the worst in everyone . . . except maybe Lisa Traymoore.*

Sam reached into her own bag and pulled out the antique white nightgown she'd covered with gold ribbons and braid. It was a wrinkled wreck. *I'm ruined,* Sam thought, sitting down heavily in a chair.

"You'd better hurry," Lisa told Sam, coming over to the mirror to fix her hair. "We're on in just a couple of minutes." She had on a beige chiffon gown with spaghetti straps, with a nude-toned lace slip under the sheer overlayer.

"Diana De Witt and Lorell Courtland stole my evening gown," Sam said, tears welling up in her eyes.

"I can't believe anyone would really do that," Lisa said kindly.

"They did, though," Sam insisted. "They're the ones who put that crap on the bottom of my jazz shoes and cut my bathing suit." She gulped hard. "And I had a great gown—I made it myself—black velvet and rhinestone pins . . ."

"Black velvet?" Lisa interrupted.

Sam nodded miserably. "It would have been hot, but worth it. See, I design my own stuff, and . . . oh, what difference does it make now?"

"Look," Lisa said, "I've got another gown here. Take it."

"Why are you being so nice to me?"

"I'm a saint," Lisa said with a laugh. "Here, just put it on." She handed Sam a red strapless fitted gown. "And hurry."

Sam scrambled into the dress while Lisa helped. "No matter what happens," Sam said, "I have to take you to lunch or dinner or something for doing this for me."

Lisa quickly zipped Sam up. "Listen, I think I know who took your gown."

"Yeah, me, too," Sam said, reaching for her compact and blotting her sweaty skin.

Then she slipped into the black heels she'd brought with her.

"No, not who you think," Lisa said. She tucked some of Sam's stray hairs back into place. "I saw Tawny Lynn Mayfair over here before, and her assigned spot is clear over on the other side of the dressing room."

"Oh, come on," Sam chided. "She doesn't even know me!"

"Yes, she does. Believe me, she keeps track of any girl she thinks might actually be competition. She's a real pageant-head," Lisa explained. "She was in another pageant I did and she got disqualified for putting black ink on another contestant's gown—someone caught her in the act. I never really believed she did it, but now I'm beginning to wonder."

"But why would she pick on me?" Sam wondered.

"I guess she thinks you might win," Lisa said with as shrug.

"But she's perfect-looking!" Sam exclaimed.

"Well, talent counts for fifty percent of

the total," Lisa reminded Sam. "Maybe she knows what a great dancer you are."

"All girls should be out in the holding area, all girls should be out in the holding area!" the assistant called, scampering through the dressing room.

"Let's go," Lisa said.

"I still can't believe—" Sam began.

"Well, it's too late to find out now," Lisa said.

Sam stood in line, waiting her turn to parade across the stage. *A red gown is not exactly what I'd put on this redhead,* Sam thought ruefully, *but at least I'm not naked.*

"Miss Tawny Lynn Mayfair!" Mrs. Spangler announced, and Tawny Lynn took her turn on the stage.

God, she looks totally perfect, Sam thought enviously. *There's no way she sabotaged my stuff. I know it was Lorell and Diana, and I'm going to find a way to prove it.*

"Ladies and gentlemen, the judges have just handed me the names of the five finalists," Mr. Spangler said. "I will read them in no particular order. If your name is called, please step forward."

Please, Sam prayed, *please let me be a finalist. Even if I did have to parade around in a clingy red gown that looked like dog meat on me, maybe there's still some hope.*

"Diana De Witt!" Mr. Spangler called.

The audience applauded and Diana moved forward, throwing a kiss to the crowd.

Die on the spot, Sam willed. *Melt like the evil witch that you are.*

"Lisa Traymoore!" Mr. Spangler called out.

I'm glad for her, Sam thought, managing to smile through her own fear. *She's terrific and she deserves it.*

"Tawny Lynn Mayfair!"

Tawny Lynn glided forward, looking like the queen of all she surveyed. She smiled radiantly at the judges, and managed to look both modest and as if all this were her due at the same time.

Okay, I didn't make it, Sam thought. *Two names left and neither one is going to be mine. I can handle it.*

189

"Samantha Bridges!"

"That's me!" Sam squeaked before she could stop herself. She walked forward to join the other three finalists, and she could hear her friends screaming her name from the crowd.

"And our last finalist is Debra Klein!" Mr. Spangler announced. Debra, a classical pianist with great high cheekbones, came forward looking happy and shocked.

"Ladies and gentlemen, a round of applause for our five finalists, one of whom will soon be crowned Miss Sunset Island!"

Sam stood in the offstage holding area with Debra Klein. Debra and Lisa had already been asked their interview question, and Tawny Lynn was on stage that very minute. Since all five girls were asked the same question, they'd all had to wait out of earshot while the others were responding.

"I can't believe I'm in the finals," Debra said, wringing her hands nervously. "I only entered this on a dare."

"From who?" Sam asked, trying to calm the butterflies in her own stomach.

"My best friend," Debra explained. "I don't have the money to finish my senior year at the Boston Conservatory of Music next year, and my friend Susannah said if I won this thing I'd have the money, and . . . oh, ignore me. I'm rambling like an idiot."

"It's okay," Sam said. "I'm feeling pretty idiotic myself right about now."

"Samantha?" the assistant called, coming for Sam.

"Why do I feel like I'm being called into the gynecologist's office or something?" Sam quipped nervously.

The assistant wasn't amused.

Sam took a deep breath, put her shoulders back, and walked regally onstage.

"Hello, Sam. Nervous?" Mr. Spangler asked her.

"Extremely," Sam admitted. "I'm not sure I remember how to speak English."

The audience laughed sympathetically. Sam smiled and felt better.

"Okay, Sam, here's the question. Who is

the woman alive today that you most admire, and why?"

I actually got the question I practiced, Sam thought giddily. *I can do this! I can ace this! I know just what to say and—*

Wait a minute. He said "the woman alive today." The alive part wasn't in Dixie's sample question. AND I HAVE NO IDEA IF MOTHER TERESA IS DEAD OR ALIVE!

All of this passed through Sam's brain in a millisecond. She gulped hard.

I can't say Mother Teresa, because if she's dead I'll look like an idiot. Help!

Just at that moment, Sam caught sight of Carrie crouched near the steps, snapping her picture. Carrie gave her a smile full of love and encouragement.

"Your answer?" Mr. Spangler prompted.

Sam turned to the mike. "The woman alive today I most admire is my best friend, Carrie Alden," she said. "She's smart, kind, and a really great friend. And she's always growing and learning, which is just what I hope to do, too."

"Thank you, Sam," Mr. Spangler said.

"Thank you," Sam said. She turned and

headed to join the other three finalists, who stood to the rear of the stage.

I totally blew it, Sam thought, still smiling.

"That was great," Lisa whispered to Sam.

"It sucked," Sam whispered back. "What did you say?"

"Hillary Clinton," Lisa whispered. "I knew it was supposed to be Mother Teresa, but I couldn't remember if she was dead or alive!"

"She's alive," Tawny Lynn said smugly from the other side of Lisa. "She was my answer."

"What did Diana say?" Sam asked.

"Norma Kamali," Lisa reported.

"A *dress designer?*" Sam replied, astounded.

"At least I know for sure she's alive," Diana snapped through her plastic smile.

At the front of the stage, Mr. Spangler had just finished asking Debra Klein the same question they'd all been asked. The audience awaited her answer.

"The woman alive today I admire the most is my mother," Debra said simply. "After my dad died from cancer she single-handedly raised me and my four older brothers. We didn't have much money, but my mom always made us feel rich. Now two of my brothers are doctors, one is an airline pilot, and one is a state senator. My mother is the kind of woman I hope to become one day."

Sam, Diana, Tawny Lynn, and Lisa all looked at one another.

They knew when they'd been beaten.

TWELVE

"And now," Mrs. Spangler said, beaming at the crowd, "while the judges are doing their final tallying, we have a very special treat for you. Since Mr. Spangler and I are new to your lovely island, we haven't heard these two young men sing before, but I understand they are the pride and joy of Sunset Island. Please welcome to our stage Billy Sampson and Pres Travis!"

"Hey!" Sam exclaimed, clutching Lisa's hand. "They're two of my best friends! They're in my band, Flirting With Danger!"

"I know," Lisa said. "I heard you guys play at the Play Café a while back. You were really great."

"Hello out there," Billy said into the mike. "I'm Billy, and this is Pres." Pres gave a quick wave and went back to tuning a string on his acoustic guitar. "You might know us from our band, Flirting With Danger—"

"Yeah!" someone in the crowd screamed enthusiastically, and there was applause and more yells of appreciation.

"Thanks," Billy said. "That means a lot to us. Uh, I've been away from the island for a while, and I can't even begin to tell you how much I missed everyone."

"We missed you, too, Billy!" someone yelled.

"Today Pres and I would like to sing a tune I wrote while I was away. I think it pretty much sums up how I feel about this island, my friends"—he looked over at Pres—"and the girl I love." He looked down at Carrie, who was standing there gazing up at him, her face aglow with happiness. "It's called 'Dreams of Home.'"

I haven't even heard this song yet, Sam thought, sitting on the edge of her seat. *This is so cool!*

Pres and Billy played a simple introduction, then they both began to sing.

196

I've traveled far from where I started
Didn't know just where I'd end.
I met a lot of folks along the way
Some that I'd call friends.

But I just kept on keeping on
Restless as a rolling stone.
Until the day I found this island
And I knew that I was home.

Home is where the heart is
Home is where you're loved
Home is where you make your
  dreams come true
Dreams of home, dreams of you.

Now, I have loved and lost before
Didn't know I'd hurt so bad.
And I have had some fine, sweet times
I've been happy, I've been sad.

But something made me wander
Something made me roam
Until the day I found this island
And I knew that I was home.

Home is where the heart is
Home is where you're loved

Home is where you make
  your dreams come true
Dreams of home, dreams of you.

"The chorus is real simple," Pres drawled
into the microphone, "so we want all of you
who love Sunset Island as much as we do to
join in. Everybody!"
And together, everyone began to sing.

Home is where the heart is
Home is where you're loved
Home is where you make your dreams
  come true
Dreams of home, dreams of you.
Dreams of home, dreams of you.
Dreams of home . . . dreams of you.

"Thank you, thank you very much!" Billy
and Pres called over the cheering of the
audience. Everyone stood up, clapping and
yelling. Sam was on her feet with the rest
of the audience—at that moment she didn't
much care how it looked. She looked down
at Carrie, who had tears streaming down

198

her face, and she had to brush away a few of her own.

Whatever happens, it was worth it just to be here to hear Billy and Pres sing that song, Sam thought.

"Thank you so much," Mrs. Spangler gushed into the microphone. "That was really wonderful. And now I believe we have the judges' decision."

Mr. Spangler picked up an envelope from Lord Owen and handed it to Mrs. Spangler.

"Fourth runner-up, and winner of a two-hundred-dollar savings bond, is . . . Diana De Witt!"

"I beat her!" Sam hissed happily to Lisa. "Whatever happens now, at least I beat her!"

"Third runner-up, and winner of a three-hundred-dollar savings bond, is . . . Lisa Traymoore!"

As Lisa came forward Sam clapped as hard as she could.

There are only three of us left, Sam realized. *I could actually win. It's actually possible.*

"Second runner-up, and winner of a

four-hundred-dollar savings bond, is . . . Samantha Bridges!"

With a smile plastered on her face, Sam moved forward. She could hear her friends screaming for her, but all she could feel was a lump of disappointment. *Stop it,* she told herself as Mrs. Spangler kissed her and handed her a bouquet of roses. *You did really well, and what's more important, you beat out Lorell and Diana!*

"Well, I know you two ladies are really nervous," Mrs. Spangler said in her unctuous voice.

Debra grabbed Tawny Lynn's hand and squeezed it hard. Tawny Lynn grabbed back, but without any conviction.

"The first runner-up, who will serve as Miss Sunset Island should the winner be unable to serve, is . . . Debra Klein!"

Debra moved forward. Tawny Lynn screamed and clapped her hands over her mouth. Once Debra got her roses she moved over to stand with Sam, Diana, and Lisa, and Tawny Lynn was presented with her crown. While everyone applauded and the photographers snapped pictures, Tawny Lynn took her royal walk around the stage.

It was finally over. Backstage was bedlam, with people laughing, screaming, and crying from relief that the whole thing was finished.

Sam saw Debra backstage. "Hey, congrats," she said.

"Oh, thanks, to you, too," Debra replied.

"I wish you had won," Sam told her. "You know, so you could afford to go back to school."

"Oh well, I never even thought I'd get this far," Debra said with a sweet smile. "You're a really talented dancer, by the way. I think the world is going to see big things from you."

"Thanks," Sam said, genuinely touched.

"Sam, come with me," Lisa demanded, marching up to Sam.

"What?"

"Don't talk, walk," Lisa said. She looked over her shoulder at Debra. "And you, don't move a muscle."

"Where are we going?" Sam asked Lisa as she followed her through the crowd, leaving a very puzzled Debra behind. "And what happened to that sweet girl you used to be?"

"I'm on a mission," Lisa replied over the noise surrounding them. She spied the same harried assistant who had worked backstage during the show and walked right up to her. "Excuse me, I need you for a moment. It's extremely urgent. Follow me."

Lisa spoke with such conviction that the assistant immediately followed her and Sam. The trio rounded the corner, and there was Tawny Lynn, surrounded by well-wishers. Lisa worked her way through the crowd.

"Tawny Lynn?" Lisa said.

"Yes?"

"Please open that dance bag," Lisa said, pointing to the large tapestry bag at Tawny Lynn's feet.

"I will not," Tawny Lynn said. "Are you crazy?"

"No, I'm not crazy," Lisa said evenly. "Just open it."

Tawny Lynn looked at the assistant. "I

guess she's upset because she lost," she said. "Please do something."

"I'm upset all right, but not because I lost," Lisa said. "I believe you cheated."

A hush fell over the crowd.

"You must be out of your mind," Tawny Lynn snapped.

"Really, Miss Traymoore, you can't just accuse—"

Lisa refused to listen. She picked up Tawny Lynn's bag and dumped out its contents. Out fell Sam's black velvet evening gown, a pair of scissors, and some lip gloss.

"*You!*" Sam cried. "Lisa was right! You cut my bathing suit and wrecked my jazz shoes!" She picked up her Samstyles evening gown. "And this is my evening gown!" She looked over at the assistant. "I *told* you someone stole it!"

"This is a total invasion of my privacy!" Tawny Lynn yelled. "I'll sue all of you!"

"I can prove it's my gown," Sam yelled back. "Look at the Samstyles label in the back. It's mine!"

The assistant picked up the velvet gown

and looked at the label. Sure enough, it said SAMSTYLES.

"They're—they're framing me!" Tawny spluttered.

"No one is framing you," Lisa said. "I saw you over near Sam's stuff, and then I saw a piece of black velvet hanging out of your bag when you walked by me before the evening gown competition. When Sam told me her gown was black velvet and it was missing, I put two and two together. I guess you really did cheat in that other pageant we were in together, huh?"

Everyone stared at Tawny Lynn.

"You won't get away with this!" she screamed. "I'm suing every single one of you!"

"What happens now?" Sam asked the assistant. "She can't win if she cheated."

"No, she can't," the assistant agreed. "I'll have to bring all of this up with the Spanglers. But I'm sure Tawny Lynn will be disqualified."

"Which means Debra will win!" Sam realized. "She'll have the money to go back to school!"

"Let's go tell her!" Lisa cried.

"You can't do this to me!" Tawny Lynn was whining as Lisa and Sam hurried off. "They're telling lies about me! I swear!"

But already the crowd around Tawny Lynn was moving away, distancing themselves from a liar and a cheat.

"Debra!" Sam cried, running over to the girl. "Tawny Lynn is going to be disqualified for cheating!"

"She cheated?" Debra asked softly.

"She did," Lisa affirmed. "And do you know what that means?"

"It means . . . I won?" Debra answered faintly.

"You won!" Sam confirmed excitedly. "I'm so happy for you! You'll have the money for school!" Sam and Lisa threw their arms around Debra.

"I—I can't believe it!" Debra said, shock and happiness colliding on her face. "I'm just so amazed!"

"Hey, this means I'm first runner-up!" Sam chortled. "If anything happens to you, I'm Miss Sunset Island!"

"Murder isn't worth it, Sam," Lisa said with a laugh.

"Listen, Lisa, you are really terrific," Sam said, turning to her. "I owe you a lot."

"I'll just take you up on that lunch sometime, okay?" Lisa said with a smile.

"You're on," Sam agreed, and she quickly wrote her number down for Lisa on a slip of paper. "Call me, okay?"

"I will," Lisa promised.

"Oh, man, I gotta go find my friends!" Sam exclaimed. "Wait until they hear I'm first in line to the throne!" She quickly gathered up all her stuff and went out into the main conference room, scanning the crowd for her friends. They were standing together in the back of the room, talking and laughing together.

"You guys are the greatest!" Sam said, running over to them.

"Samantha Bridges, you were wonderful," Pres said, wrapping his arms around her. "You did me proud, girl."

Sam kissed him quickly and hugged him hard. "Right back atcha, big guy," she whispered to him. She turned and grinned happily at all her friends. "I had so much fun!"

"Sam, I have to tell you, you are one hell of a dancer," X said, giving Sam a hug.

"I can't believe you stayed to see me dance!" Sam cried, hugging him back.

"I wouldn't have missed it for the world!"

"You were pretty good, Sam," Becky said, "but why were you wearing that red thing for the evening gown competition?"

"Yeah," Allie agreed. "No offense, but it really sucked on you."

Sam laughed. "It's a long story—I'll tell you later."

Out of the corner of her eye, Sam saw Lorell and Diana leaving the conference room. "You guys, wait right here, I'll be right back," Sam said.

She dashed across the room to Lorell and Diana. "Hey, I want to talk to you guys."

They turned around. "I suppose you want to laugh at me," Lorell said furiously. "X just told me the truth about himself. Everything you told me was a lie."

"You're right," Sam admitted. "I'm busted."

"Is that supposed to be an apology?"

"No," Sam said. "I thought the whole

207

thing was a riot and you deserved it. Hey, you're not gonna stop payment on the checks to his ballet company, are you?"

"No," Lorell said. "I happen to like him as a person." She got a coquettish look on her face. "Besides, maybe I can be the woman to change his mind about his sexual orientation."

"Let's go, Lorell," Diana said. "Muffy Sue and the rest of your family are waiting in front of the building. I'm afraid she's going to break into a tap number from *Annie* if we don't show up soon."

"Wait," Sam said.

"What?" Diana asked with exasperation. "You want to accuse us of stealing your gown again or something?"

"No," Sam replied. "I want to apologize to you. I know now that it wasn't you two who did all that stuff."

Diana's mouth dropped open. "You're *apologizing* to us?"

"That's what I just said," Sam agreed.

"Gee, let me put this one on my calendar in red ink," Diana sneered. "Samantha Bridges actually admits she was wrong."

"I was," Sam said. "I'm sorry."

Diana cocked her head to one side and looked at Sam. "You know, I think you really mean it."

"I do," Sam said.

Diana stared at Sam a moment. "Well, then, thanks," she finally said. "Come on, Lorell." And with one last look at Sam, she walked away.

Wow, no nasty comment, Sam thought as she rushed back to her friends. *Maybe it's a miracle!*

A good hundred feet away from her friends, she stopped. There was Emma with Kurt's arm around her, Carrie and Billy holding hands, and Pres putting away his guitar. Jake was tickling Erin, and Jay was talking with Molly and Darcy. The twins, Dixie, and Tori were huddled around X, getting his autograph.

I love these people so much, Sam realized, taking it all in. *They mean the world to me. Billy's song was right—Sunset Island really is home. Home is where you are accepted just the way you are. Home is where you are loved.*

With that thought Sam wiped a tear of happiness from her eye, and she walked toward the people she loved, heading for home.

SUNSET ISLAND MAILBOX

Dear Readers,

I really hope you all read and enjoyed the previous Sunset book. My editor told me that Sunset Fantasy is the funniest thing that she's ever read in her life. Jeff read it and he agrees! So check it out—if you haven't already!

News from Nashville: Lately, I've been hard at work on a new play. It's funny, but it's about a serious subject: an American teenage girl who denies that the Nazis tried to exterminate Jews during the Second World War. Its title is Anne Frank & Me, and the world premiere will be in April, 1995, here in Nashville.

There are some things that are just indisputable facts in this world, and it is up to all of us to defend the truth. The earth is round. There is no cure for AIDS yet. And the Nazis did have gas chambers where they murdered Jews.

Many readers have written in to say that they've gotten their younger sisters into the Club Sunset Island books, and that they're enjoying the new series too! That's great. I love writing those books and hope that the new series goes on forever.

I've got a new bulletin board up for photos in my office. In last week's batch of mail—157 letters—I got 27 photos. Yes! Keep 'em coming.

See you on the island!
Best-
Cherie Bennett

Cherie Bennett
c/o General Licensing Company
24 West 25th Street
New York, New York 10010

Dear Cherie,
Let me start by saying that I am absolutely crazy about your books. I'm seventeen years old. I started reading your books about three years ago. I also enjoy reading the Ocean City series. I find that the author's writing is very similar to yours. I would love to meet you, but would you ever come to Canada?
            Karla Myrstol
            Burlington, Ontario

Dear Karla,

I love my Canadian fans! And there are a lot of them—probably ten percent of my fan mail comes from Canada, which is too cool. There is a chance that one of my plays will be produced in Winnipeg soon, which isn't exactly near Ontario, I know. The Ocean City series came after Sunset Island and just goes to show that when someone has a success, like we have with Sunset Island, someone else will try to copy it! Accept no substitutes!

Best,
Cherie

Dear Cherie,

Thanks for writing back. I'm really glad we might be able to meet someday. I have two questions. The main one is: Do you know R. L. Stine? He is my other favorite author. The second one is: When is your birthday? I would like to know so I can send you a card!

Your #1 reader (really),
Lauren Mandel
Mahwah, NJ

Dear Lauren,

My birthday is October 6th. Jeff's is August 7th. I do know R. L. Stine! We met recently in California, and though I'd like to say that he's as horrible and ghoulish and terrorizing as his books are, he's not scary at all in person!

Best,
Cherie

Dear Cherie,

I've written before, but after reading your last few books, I felt compelled to write again. I suddenly realized how your characters are so similar to my two best friends and me. I sent you a photo a couple of years ago, but here's another one that will bring you up to date!

Sincerely,
Elizabeth Weiss
Houtzdale, PA

Dear Elizabeth,

Great to hear from you again. A lot of readers find that they have two friends who make their trio like Sam, Emma, and Carrie. Thanks for the new photo! Several other readers, including Torrey Mandell, Amy Johnstonbaugh, and Jackie Fleming have also sent me photo updates. And you all are total cuties!

Best,
Cherie